Books are to be returned on or before
the last date below.

1 3 SEP 2007

1 8 OCT 2007

1 8 MAR 2011

2 6 OCT 2007

2 1 JAN 2008

- 4 SEP 2009

1 9 MAR 2010

2 5 MAR 2013

PAC
3/13

1 7 AUG 2007

7 SEP 07

ALLBEURY, T.
The networks

**CORNWALL COUNTY COUNCIL
LIBRARY SERVICES**

THE NETWORKS

Recent Titles by Ted Allbeury from Severn House

BERLIN EXCHANGE

COLD TACTICS

NEVER LOOK BACK

RULES OF THE GAME

SPECIAL FORCES

THE NETWORKS

Ted Allbeury

severn
House

This title first published in Great Britain 2002 by °
SEVERN HOUSE PUBLISHERS LTD of
9–15 High Street, Sutton, Surrey SM1 1DF,
complete with new Introduction by the author.
Originally published in 1975 in Great Britain under
the title *The Special Collection.*
This title first published in the USA 2003 by
SEVERN HOUSE PUBLISHERS INC of
595 Madison Avenue, New York, N.Y. 10022.

British Library Cataloguing in Publication Data

Allbeury, Ted, 1917-
    The networks
    1. World War, 1939-1945 - Secret service - Great Britain - Fiction
    2. Suspense fiction
    I.   Title
    823.9'14 [F]

    ISBN 0-7278-5898-X

Printed and bound in Great Britain by
MPG Books Ltd., Bodmin, Cornwall.

With love to Graz

I had needed secretarial help for a week and I phoned a local agency. They said that Miss Felinska would arrive in an hour. I didn't know then that was to be the last hour before my life was radically changed. When I opened the door for Miss Felinska I greeted her in my modest Italian and she amiably informed me that her origins were Polish, not Italian.

She was stunningly beautiful and she was twenty-two. Her full name was Grazyna Maria Felinska. I was fifty-two and less than a year later we were married. We were married for thirty years. The happiest years of my rather disjointed life.

She quietly and lovingly made our life a pleasure, and my writing owes much more than I can say to her influence. She was more intellectual than I am and got an OU Honours degree while bringing up our children. A great reader with wide taste and a laughing, loving disposition. I hated having sometimes to be away from her, and my family still laugh about me phoning Gatwick on my way to give the Bertold Brecht lecture in Berlin and telling Graz that I was coming back instead of catching the plane.

In my time with Graz I wrote over forty novels and a lot of radio plays. Sadly for me Graz died just over two years ago. I haven't written anything since. I miss her all the time. She was the magic.

Ted Allbeury, 2002

PART ONE

Chapter 1

There were two pistols lying on the green baize table-top and the armourer-sergeant watched the tall man as he stood looking from one to the other. One was a Luger PO8 and the other a Walther MP. Both were 9 mm parabellum cartridge types and the fine film of oil that covered them had marked the green baize.

For a month the tall man had been shooting 98s at 25 metres with the Walther. In the same month he'd been shooting 95s with the Luger. He preferred the Luger. It had a better feel as it lay in his hand. It even looked more like a gun should look than the blown-up version of the Walther PP. But he knew from past experience that the Luger had too many stoppages. Mud and sand seemed to have what could literally be a fatal attraction for Luger mechanisms. It said a lot for the Luger that he even hesitated in his choice, yet as any gunman will tell you, firing on a practice range is one thing and doing it for real is another. Then, 'feel' matters a lot. Without any hesitation he reached forward and touched the Walther. 'I'll take this one, sergeant.'

He had fired another forty-eight rounds after the pistol had been recalibrated and the acrid stench of cordite seemed to go with him as he walked up the basement steps to the street. He walked slowly across Green Park, down towards Hyde Park Corner, and then he turned into the back streets that lead to Shepherd Market. The man standing in the foyer of the Curzon Cinema bent down to release the door-lock. As he opened the door he said, 'Morning captain, Major Franks is already in there.'

There was a still picture on the screen of the front page of the previous day's copy of the *Berliner Tageblatt*, and a voice on the sound system was saying crisply but with a slight lisp, 'Und hier sind die heutige Nachrichten zu Deutsch . . .' As he slid into the comfortable seat alongside Franks he said, 'Why does that stupid bastard always say "zu" instead of auf"?'

Franks laughed softly. 'Mainly to annoy you, I think.'

3

They settled down to hear recordings of the morning's news bulletins as broadcast by the radio stations in Berlin, Hamburg and Munich. They were shown two current German news-reels and news-reels from occupied France and Holland. After a long but currently popular version of *Die Lustige Witwe* in rather poor colour, there was a short pause, and the speaker system announced that they were to be shown a film made two months previously by special order for the Führer's private viewing. There was no commentary to the film, just a pleasant piano accompaniment as twenty or so very pretty girls did callisthenics. Most of the girls were blondes and all of them were naked. The new 300 mm Schneider telelens lingered lovingly and unashamedly on jiggling breasts and youthful bellies. When the film finished the speakers crackled again and a man with a fruity Berlin accent retailed three of the latest dirty jokes circulating in Germany. All were political and one was funny.

Going from the darkness of the cinema into the bright December sunshine they shaded their eyes as they looked for a taxi. It was the 20th of December 1944 and Captain Felinski was parachuting into Germany in four days' time.

The first approach to Felinski had been made in May, and they'd spent almost a month before that, checking through the SOE and MI6 records for suitable candidates. There had been three 'possibles' but Felinski's Russian and Polish had outweighed some missing qualifictions.

Despite his name, Felinski was third-generation English. His great-grandfather was a victim of that fateful year 1830, when the revolution in Paris had decided the fate of France. The hatreds of that revolution blew their seeds to Brussels and broke up the uneasy kingdom of the Netherlands, and there had been flames enough to spare for Polish officers and landowners to fling their hopeless challenge to Tzar Nicholas and the Russian Empire. It was a year before the flames were stamped out, and with them the last vestige of Polish liberty.

From 1831, Paris became the intellectual capital of the Poles. Stefan Felinski was not an intellectual and he had brought his wife and small son to England, where his talents as one of the finest horse-breeders and trainers in Europe were used on a farm in East Anglia. At the end of ten years he had bought a farm and developed the most successful breeding establishment for work horses in the four counties. His son had added another thousand acres to the farm by the time his grandson was born. Stephen Felinski was twenty-one on the day the Germans invaded Poland in 1939, and he'd joined the British Army the day before war was declared.

In Central Intelligence Records they had thousands of simple punched cards and in May 1944 something remarkably like a large knitting needle had been pushed through the holes in a data check card, and when it was lifted its catch was three record cards of men with a long list of vices and virtues that would make them suitable subjects to be dropped in enemy territory and sustain themselves with minimum help until the war with Germany was over. The Joint Intelligence Committee's estimate was that that would be in another seven months.

When British Security decides on such an operation, once the man has been selected, his briefing, training and support are relentlessly efficient. The first approach to Felinski had been oblique. He was given two weeks at the British Embassy in Stockholm as an adviser to King Gustav's royal stables on a breeding and training plan for the next ten years. The King was also receiving advice from German and American experts at the same time. It was a pleasant, civilized interlude but it left Felinski puzzled as to the real purpose of the two weeks' jaunt. His knowledge of horse-breeding was very limited.

Immediately on his return to London he was asked if he would be willing to be dropped into Germany on a special mission. There had been no hesitation and he'd reported at Ringway, just outside Manchester, the same evening. He didn't make a good parachutist despite the extra days that they tacked on to the standard course, but they came to the conclusion that he was competent enough for what was going to be a single operational drop.

There were two days in a dentist's chair while his fillings were removed and replaced with their Germanic equivalents. An appendix scar was checked and a barely visible operation scar on his rib-cage was cut and resewn with continental stitches. And finally his hair had been cut *en brosse*.

From that point he had lived in the two rooms of a basement flat in Lancaster Gate where everything – plumbing, furniture, carpets, décor, switches, appliances and utensils – were all German. He was forbidden to listen to any radio stations other than Berlin, Hamburg and Munich. Each day he received two German newspapers, one day old, from the Lisbon Embassy. He was probably the worst informed of His Majesty's Intelligence officers. He was allowed no contact with English-speaking people outside a handful of service personnel.

On the top floor of the Peter Robinson store at Oxford Circus there were long corridors with doors to small offices which were air-conditioned and heavily sound-proofed. It was here that the specialists of Security Signals transmitted and received the radio traffic to agents in enemy-occupied Europe. And it was here that Felinski was trained to use a Morse key, and a code based on the date and the letters of the first two lines of a song by Charles Trenet called 'Il pleut dans ma chambre'. When they had seen his lack of skill with a soldering iron they had pulled the small transceiver apart and converted most of the soldered joints to crocodile clips. The girl who was going to handle his traffic worked hard with him to improve his operating technique and worked even harder trying to decide whether she was in love with the man or the glamour and danger of his assignment.

For the last three months he had spent an hour each day at Drury Lane Theatre in which there was a row of shops in the auditorium where he purchased his food and supplies at current German prices using the appropriate coupons. His food was limited to the standard German rations. Much time was given to the details of his cover story, and in the studio backstage there was further intensive language tuition.

Twice a week he attended briefing meetings at one of MI6's cover addresses. This was usually the MGM offices in St James's Street where girls in twin-sets and pearls acted as lion-tamers to some of the security services' wilder elements. At the first of these meetings he'd been handed photographs and maps of the dropping zone together with the dossier of the man who was to give him cover in Germany. When he opened the packet of photographs he had recognized the German expert he had met at the Swedish royal stables. Baron von Leder was an internationally famous horseman and had led the German team at equestrian events all over the world, including the Olympics.

6

His horsemanship and charm had made him friends all over the world, and this popularity had allowed him to stand clear of the Nazis and still survive. He never discussed them favourably or unfavourably, either in public or private. Although he had admired their courage he had been dismayed by the ineptness and insecurity of the group who came to be known as the 20th of July plotters. When Hitler had hung them from meat-hooks in Berlin he had shuddered at their fate but not for a moment did he turn from the path he had chosen. And in England the plans and the training went on, and for the first time Felinski was given an inkling of what his mission would be in Germany. At that meeting the DDMI, the Deputy Director of Military Intelligence, had, without any intention of humour, said drily to Felinski and the others, 'And if you get yourself killed before the surrender we shall have wasted our time.'

Chapter 2

The briefing meeting took place at the 'safe' house in Ebury Street. Felinski and Franks sat in the smaller room and three senior SIS men and an SOE officer were assembled in the larger room with files and photographs.

There was a photograph of the Royal Family at Balmoral on the long sideboard and on the wall facing the window was a Sisley water-colour, not a good one. On the wall facing Felinski was a Munnings, and his good English heart was warmed by the bright shafts of sunlight shining on a glossy chestnut. But blood will out and some leftover chromosome from his Polish great-grandfather made him notice that the stallion was down on his pasterns with a bad tail set-on into the bargain.

The ATS girl brought in coffee and although she appeared to ignore Felinski he sensed that she was examining him. When she had gone Franks leaned back, pushed his empty cup forward on the table and crossed his legs at the ankles. He had a thin, ascetic face, was in his middle thirties, and was almost completely bald. Once again Felinski wondered how Franks had got into this rough, tough business and what his special qualities were.

'Well now, Stephen, let me put you in the picture. I'll give you the general outline first and then we can fill in the details. Agreed?' Felinski nodded but he didn't speak, and Franks continued.

'Baron von Leder, as you know, will provide you with physical cover. You will be his business and agricultural adviser. The man he had before died six months ago. As you know the Baron is assisting us because he's an anti-Nazi. He's never been anything else and we've had contact with him since about 1935, through Stockholm of course. But you must not look for anything more than physical shelter from him, to ask more than that would not only be unfair but highly dangerous. Your cover has been specifically designed to leave him in the clear if you are picked up. At that point he would rely on you for protection. Just as up to that point you have relied on him. Understood?'

'Is this laid down by him?'

'Not at all. It's laid down by us. He is of great value to us and will be most important after the war. We would sacrifice a lot to preserve him intact.' Franks looked across to check Felinski's reaction, but there was none visible.

'Now the small group you are going to join are Russian.' He noticed the surprise on Felinski's face but he ignored it, closing his eyes as if to blot out anything that might divert his thoughts or hinder his words.

'They are badly trained and considerably demoralized. They have a source which is proving very valuable – I'd better say potentially valuable, because it's coming out far too late at the moment to be of use.'

'Have we got any details of the source?'

'Yes. It's inside the Gauleitung at Hanover. The Gauleiter's secretary as a matter of fact. She's providing political and military information. Most of it is only a day old when she hands it over, but by the time they get it out it's pretty useless.'

'No radio?'

'We understand it was damaged when they landed.'

'Landed? How landed?'

'By parachute. Nearly a year ago. The Russians seem to have been rather ham-fisted. They dropped a large number of Russian nationals in 1943. Most of them were picked up in days. Inadequate documents, poor cover stories and insufficient training. The rest were picked up over the next six months. One of them, named Voronov, was never picked up. He still had a radio and was in contact with the Moscow Centre until three months ago. Then for some reason they ignored his call-sign. He went on net at the right time every day for eight weeks. There's some indication from Geneva that the Russians think he's blown or turned. We are pretty sure he's not. We think that like the others he was badly trained and can't repair the radio. The stuff he is sending out is high-grade and we want it, but we need it fast, by radio.'

'How's it coming out now?'

'He's got a long-winded contact to SOE. He gets it to Liège and then it goes to Bruges and it takes over three weeks on average. It also overloads the SOE Signals net in Belgium.'

'Who are the rest of them?'

'All Russian but a more recent vintage. The Moscow Centre dropped another swarm of parachute agents about six months ago. Just as badly equipped and trained as the first lot. Three of them ended by being shuffled along to Voronov. We think the remnants of the German communist party put them in touch.'

'The Moscow Centre has just left them to rot?'

'We think so.'

'Why?'

'We're not sure. One of the reasons may be that the Centre is getting first-class service on Germany from a network in Switzerland. It looks like they suspected Voronov way back. Normally they'd check on an agent they suspended, especially one of their own nationals. They'd find out one way or the other. If they finally found him turned or it was unresolved, they'd knock him off.'

'Tell me about Voronov.'

'There isn't much, but all we've got has been assembled for you. It's next door.'

'What's the pay-off for the Gauleiter's secretary?'

'She sleeps with Voronov. As you'll see he's a big bear of a man. Gauleiter Lauterbacher's a small man, maybe she likes 'em big and rough.'

'No indications, I presume, that the girl is planting stuff for the Germans.'

Franks pursed his lips and stretched slowly. 'It's been carefully gone over, Stephen – there's no indication that it's a plant.'

'You said that there are others in the group. Are they getting anything themselves or is it just Voronov?'

'We haven't much information about them. Our impression is that they are more of a nuisance than an asset. But one of them takes the stuff down to Liège – the stuff that Voronov gets from the girl. He makes contact with the SOE group down there and as I said it comes to us through SOE channels. Because we can't overload the radio operator most of it has to come by Lysander whenever we land people or supplies. Now we are moving across towards Germany our contact is almost certain to break down.'

'Why are they prepared to pass it to us?'

'For payment and some personal arrangements for Voronov – his parents are in Leningrad. Our people in Moscow keep an eye on them for him. Voronov and his chaps are stuck there anyway.'

'Does any of the stuff Voronov gets affect the Russians?'

'Yes, there's quite a lot of political stuff covering the German communists and relationships with other groups, including people in Moscow.'

'And the Russians still won't support Voronov.'

'They don't get that material.'

'Why not?'

'On military material they are well served by Geneva. The other material is political and it is not in our interest to pass it on.'

'What is my brief then?'

Franks stood up and lit a cigarette before continuing. 'We want you to pull this group together – give leadership and get the stuff back to us immediately by radio. It's our most reliable source of information on morale inside the Nazi Party and the general public, and Hanover is now the key to most troop movements in North Germany. What we are getting is high-class material but it's too late to be useful – most of it anyway. And we want to get a picture of the local communists who are actively helping the Russians.'

'Does the Russian group know I'm coming?'

'Not right now but they'll be told nearer the time.' He looked at Felinski for a moment and then said, 'I'd better make clear that you won't necessarily be welcome.'

Felinski spent ten days going over the dossiers assembled on the group. There was almost nothing on the three Russians who had recently arrived, and not much on Voronov. But what was coming out of the Hanover Gauleitung was white-hot.

There were daily situation reports from both the west and east fronts including Wehrmacht orders-of-battle. There were lists of persons arrested by the local Gestapo covering all northern Germany, and extracts of interrogations were frequently included. Daily reports from the Abwehr Aussenstelle at Hamburg and Hanover had been much reduced after the arrest of Canaris, but their assessment of civilian morale in the northern half of Germany gave invaluable information. There was much detail of the reduced rail and road facilities due to the Allied bombing campaign. There was secret correspondence between Gauleiter Lauterbacher and Himmler – and similar correspondence with Goering and Walter Schellenberg. Felinski could well understand the importance attached to this source of high-grade material. There was little doubt in his mind that the information was not planted. The crude internal treacheries revealed in the Gauleiter's private correspondence could never have been faked.

At the end of the briefing period Felinski had sat in his small flat writing a dozen non-committal letters to be forwarded to his mother while he was away. His home cover was an extended trip to Africa, and that seemed only to emphasize the operation's unreality as his letters tried to give an impression of heat and sunshine as he wrote them in a grey London pounded by V1s and V2s. He gave them unsealed to Franks.

Chapter 3

There was a warm yellow light from big hangar doors and then the doors closed behind them, and Franks walked him over to a small shack that was set in a fenced-off area of the gaunt building. Mechanics were working on an aircraft, and their voices, and the noise of tools on metal, echoed and hung in the vast roof space. Felinski noticed that the shack was not just fenced off but covered in a wire-mesh cage. At the metal door a sergeant of the RAF Police stood guard and a CSM of Field Security checked their documents. He read every word carefully, and frequently looked at their faces, checking the detailed descriptions. Finally he nodded to the sergeant and they both saluted as Franks and Felinski went through the door.

As Franks closed the door Felinski looked around the small room. It was warm and brightly lit with wall-to-wall carpet but no windows. There was a bath and shower unit along one wall. As he looked at Franks the Major waved him to one of the chairs and he moved to it and sat down.

'Stephen, we now have to go through a very precise drill. I'm sure you'll understand it's all for your benefit. But from past experience I know that it's rather depressing, so if at the end you feel a bit low you're being quite normal. I don't know for sure what causes it and we'd be particularly interested in your views in due course. Shall we start?'

And already they had started. Felinski was momentarily flattered that they wanted his opinion and then inordinately deflated at the 'in due course'. That meant it was intended to flatter and they were indifferent to his view. But he looked across at Franks and nodded.

'I'm ready when you are.'

'Right then. Take off all your clothes and put them on the trestle table over there.'

When his socks came off and he stood naked, Franks told him to bath and then take a shower. After he had towelled himself dry a medical orderly had scrubbed his fingers and toes and carried out a pedicure. Then Franks had opened the door to the adjoining room and when they went in there were hangers and hooks with his German civilian clothes. Franks sat in one of the comfortable easy chairs and was silent while Felinski dressed. For the next half hour Felinski's equipment was checked piece by piece and the radio was tested live back to London. The girl on the top floor of Peter Robinson seemed a long way away but the check came back clearly and crisply.

There was a tray of food brought in by a Field Security sergeant and Felinski took the good chicken soup and some brown toast. When he had finished he leaned back in his chair. Franks was sorting out documents on the table and when he saw that Felinski had finished eating he separated the documents one by one and identified them individually as he handed them over to him. Then they both sat, chatting of friends and fellows until an RAF squadron leader came in. He walked over to the table and spread out charts and maps, and as they stood with him he chatted easily and expertly without introducing himself.

'The Met report is fine. Very little head-wind and clear as day above the cloud layer. There's a good moon and there are over sixty planned bombing raids tonight, most of them from the UK, so the ack-ack will have plenty to occupy their minds. Now I want you to absorb the main details of this course in case anything should go wrong. I'll keep you in the picture as we go along but it'll help if I can gen you up on the flight plan. We're not going the usual route to Hanover; we're going to be fifteen minutes ahead of some Yanks who are heading for Kiel and when we get to this island here, called Fehmarn, we shall head almost due south. There are raids on Hanover and Brunswick and we shall come straight down the middle between the two towns. And about here at Celle, we shall go for a triangulation that a Pathfinder unit will lay on. The raids will have been on for about twenty-two minutes before we arrive, and everybody will be very busy. If we're dead on time you'll be down on the ground saying "Happy Christmas" just after midnight. Now have you got any questions?'

Felinski pointed at the map. 'I thought that there were heavy ack-ack batteries just south of Hanover here.'

The RAF officer raised his eyebrows. 'Well done. The map

14

boys would be very pleased with you. The batteries are well south of Hanover just outside the railway station at Salzgitter. They're mobiles mounted on railway rolling stock. That means that these particular guns are not really all that mobile. They cover an area that's either roughly north-east or south-west, and the way they point 'em depends on whether there's a raid on Berlin or not. If we're banging them in Berlin they like to lay a curtain to catch our chaps on the way back, and the mobiles cover the north-east, so that if we try to slide between Brunswick and Magdeburg then we get this lot up our arses just as we begin to relax. So they'll be pointing at Berlin tonight for the benefit of US Fifth Air Force. And that leaves you clear.'

And that was that. They synchronized watches and there were twenty minutes to go. It was after five minutes that Felinski started trembling. Suddenly it seemed unbelievable that it was going to happen. In a few hours he would be in Germany, and all the training would work or fail, but all the structure of support would be gone. In a few seconds the trembling developed into a body-shaking ague and when he found the courage to look at Franks he saw sympathy and encouragement. Franks had said quietly, 'Don't bother about me. It's always like this with everybody. Pretend I'm not here because when you're in the plane it'll go. They all say that.'

Franks looked across at Felinski for he knew that he had more reason to tremble than the others, who could be supported and, if necessary, picked up. They fell among friends. Then he used what he'd been keeping back for these last few minutes. 'By the way, your posting as a major was in today's Part Two orders. Congratulations.'

And Felinski was young enough for it to matter. As he opened his mouth to speak the door opened and the squadron leader was saying 'OK. We're off.' Franks seemed unaware of the airman and he took a deep breath.

'Major Felinski, I have to inform you that you are free to stand down from this mission and I am ordered to point out that you enter this arrangement of your own free will, not from a direct order. What do you say?'

The formal speech to ensure that HM Government would not have to pay undue compensation to the deceased's next-of-kin broke Felinski's tensions, and he laughed for the first time. He

15

picked up his four packages and said to Franks, 'Bullshitters to the last. See you when it's over.' And he moved easily to the door. At the door he turned and Franks felt that he looked very young. Too young. 'Tell them I appreciate the promotion – I really do.' And then he had turned and the door had closed.

There were four other air-crew members in the outer room and sitting stiff and upright on an RAF-issue wooden chair was the sergeant WAAF who always assembled his 'chute pack. When the squadron leader beckoned to the girl she stood up, and the sergeant helped her carry over the pack. Because of his load an oversize canopy had been made up, and he noticed that all the harness straps had been dyed dark brown and the buckles were dull black. He had leaned slightly forward as they adjusted the pack across his shoulders. The leg straps for his equipment were left loose because they were to be fitted during the flight. One of the air-crew carried his equipment and the little group wound awkwardly towards the hangar door.

Outside it was black and then, as his pupils dilated, he saw the plane. It was a Dakota and there was a wooden ladder to the door. They steadied him from behind as the weight on his back kept him unbalanced. He hated going out of Dakotas because it meant going out of the door at the side, and as you stood there with the plane lurching you could see for miles over 180°. It was nauseating and unnerving, and the jump from the fuselage always seemed too short as the wind pushed your body back into the slip-stream. He looked above the door to see if there was a clip for an automatic release wire; the squadron leader saw his look and, grinning, he pointed at the plane's belly. There it was, a proper jumping hatch complete with auto-clip and rubber-padded perimeter. It was like the milk and biscuit by his bedside at night when he was a little boy. Somebody cared about their very own coward.

The plane shuddered as both engines were taken up to top revs and then there had been a waving green light and pale, intent faces. Somebody waved as they moved forward and by the time they were airborne it was just darkness and noise.

All the Dakota's interior had been stripped out and the navigator had a whole panel of extra instruments and a comfortable working area. There was a long metal seat running

16

down the port side with loose air cushions and belts. Felinski had to ride side-saddle to accommodate his parachute pack. An RAF sergeant came back after about half an hour to help him fasten his equipment packs to his legs and as he was fastening the last buckle the plane banked sharply and the sergeant looked up quickly. 'It's all OK sir. We've just passed the island and we're turning through ninety degrees. Won't be long now.'

The navigator was busy again at his desk and Felinski could hear him on the intercom giving new bearings to the pilot. Almost an hour later the co-pilot took over and the squadron leader came back. 'Well, soldier, we've had a nice quiet journey. We're on target in ten minutes. We can see fires at Hanover and Brunswick. We may pick up a bit of flak but it won't be serious.' He put his hand on Felinski's knee. 'I don't know what you're going to do chum, but we'll be thinking of you when we get back to base.' He stood up. 'I'll be despatcher. Whoops, we must be coming down for you now.' He bent and turned the three clamps and looked at the navigator who adjusted his head-set and then held up his hand. He looked towards the squadron leader and nodded. The officer bent and put his hands on both grips and lifted, and the circular cover came up with a rush of cold air. With his mouth against Felinski's ear he said, 'Sit on the mark now. I'll tap you once for warning, and then I'll tap you twice. Then you go. Best of British and Happy Christmas.'

As Felinski settled on the white spot he looked up, and the navigator was showing three fingers. Then he pulled down the top two joints of one finger for two thousand five hundred. When the navigator showed only two fingers Felinski felt the tap on his right hand, then almost immediately two taps. He straightened and as he felt the cold air on his legs he knew he was out.

Chapter 4

The release cord jerked him slightly, there was the sudden brief pull of the slip-stream, and then the sky was silent and empty. The Dakota was far away and barely audible. What seemed like faint engine noise could be the pulse of his heart. The heavy pack was balanced by the equipment on his legs but he felt a tendency for his body to yaw, and he decided to risk the extra observation time from the ground and reduce the free-fall time. The pilot 'chute was out and then the main 'chute flapped, billowed and filled with a double thud, and his legs came down fast, with their extra weight dragging him down almost vertically. Then his eyes were accustomed to the darkness and to the north-west he could see the flickering reflection of orange flames on the clouds, and the criss-crossing of searchlights with the stabbing flashes of anti-aircraft guns. Even as he looked there were dull thuds as another stick of bombs was dropped. It must be Hanover and the raid still on. He looked across to the north-east and farther away he could see the reflection of fires in Brunswick. Then as he rushed lower he could feel the vibration in his ears, the pressure waves of the guns and bombs.

There was a glint of water in moonlight and his mind raced over the model of the dropping zone. He didn't remember any area of water and then he could see moonlight and shadows; the ground rushed up and as he hit and rolled forward the shock jarred his back. The pain was intense and he couldn't get up to spill the air from the canopy. One of the containers had come free from his leg and he was being dragged over the hard ground as a slight wind kept the canopy filled. Then suddenly he was still.

His head and his body ached, and as he lay there an owl hooted. He could hear birds fluttering uneasily in the trees because of the disturbance. He freed himself slowly from the heavy harness and saw that the canopy had been caught and held by a bush on the edge of a wood. The moonlight was very bright and he hurried to pull the canopy to the ground. He folded the parachute clumsily into the pack and pushed it deep in the bush with his equipment. As he stood up he thought he heard a dog bark, and he froze; and then as the bark was repeated he knew it was a fox. A dog fox insisting on his territory.

His watch was already set for Central European Time. It was ten past midnight. Christmas Day.

He paced out the edge of the wood; it was 300 metres and on its southern edge it went off on a wide angle. Then he knew where he was and it was nearly three miles from the nearest point of the dropping zone. The drop had been calculated for normal drift but despite the extra large canopy the heavy equipment had closed the angle of drift almost completely, and it had made an error of at least four miles.

He found the road almost immediately and followed it, keeping to the ditches and hedges till it came to the crossroads to Hildesheim. It seemed almost as bright as day. In both directions the road was dead straight and anyone crossing could be seen easily for a quarter of a mile in each direction. He lay silent in the ditch, his head lifted to look through the stalks of frozen cow parsley. There was no longer a hedge behind him, only ditches marked the edges of the fields. To his right was a signpost. The directions had been painted out but he knew where he was as if he'd lived there for months.

The road glittered with frost and the metallic surface would give off sound even better than the sparkling light. He already had one shoe off and was unlacing the other when he heard a stone clatter. He lay still, and watched and listened. After ten minutes he lifted his head to look and as he did a stone hit the road and whirred past his head. He flattened to the earth. He wouldn't be able to carry out the original contact procedure but it had been arranged that if the reception misfired he would not acknowledge anything except the last stage of the coded ritual. Flying stones were not part of that ritual, but whoever was throwing stones must have seen him and if they were outsiders they wouldn't be going through this sort of routine.

He slowly raised his head again, and almost at once he heard someone whistle softly the tune of 'Hörst du mein heimliches Rufen . . .' – until after a few bars it stopped. He looked across the road in front of him and then turned quickly as he heard footsteps coming from his right. There was someone walking slowly down the road towards him. A few yards away whoever it was stopped, but he could see nothing as they were against the light. And then a voice said softly in German: 'Wer singt "Stille Nacht" heute?' and automatically, just as he'd practised so many times, he said 'Ich heisse Bing Crosby.' The figure came forward hand outstretched, and then clambered down into the ditch. It was Baron von Leder and he whispered, 'I saw you for a moment coming down, I knew you'd miss the dropping zone so I came over. Are you all right?'

'Yes, but I've had to hide the equipment.'

'We must get it now because it's going to snow and if we leave it it will have to stay there for days, otherwise we shall leave tracks. Are you fit to walk again?'

It was nearly two hours later before they were approaching the farm. It was the deep dark patch before the first, false dawn and already there were spasmodic swirls of snow. They went past the tall dark walls of a barn and came to a door that gave on to a small courtyard alongside the wide main entrance to the main farm buildings and the big house. It was just like the model in the briefing room.

Von Leder put his mouth to Felinski's ear and whispered, 'I'm taking you to the gamekeeper's cottage. Do you remember where it is?' Felinski nodded, and they set off slowly and carefully following a post-and-rail fence. Where the fence ended, the path entered a wood, and two hundred yards farther on they came to the cottage. Inside there were the glowing remnants of a log fire, and as they stood there von Leder shone a small torch across the floor and on each of the walls. It was just one large room, with a toilet and bathroom cut off by pine planks.

Von Leder said quietly, 'Let us put your equipment away before we talk.' There were old-fashioned russet quarry tiles in the bathroom and with a knife von Leder eased up a section of four tiles which gave access to a metal-clad sump. There was ample room for the equipment and the parachute pack.

Back in the main room von Leder put two logs on the fire and they sat facing one another across the stone hearth.

'There is food for you in the cupboard. Not very much I'm afraid, but before you eat I shall have to tell you that the first part of the plan has been ruined. You were to come here as if from the train from Berlin that gets to the Hanover Station at a few minutes before midnight. The train never arrived because of the air-raid. So what do you want to do about your cover?'

'Where did it stop?'

'I've no idea.'

Felinski had been briefed on that train journey in detail. It was the first link in his cover story that provided authenticity. With that gone his story would always be suspect under deep interrogation.

'Is there a telephone here at the cottage?'

Von Leder nodded and turned to point, 'It's on the bracket by the door.'

'I'll need to find out where the train stopped and what happened. Did the passengers disperse? Was any alternative transport offered?'

Von Leder stood up and walked across the room. It was an old-fashioned telephone with a handle to crank to call the operator. He waited for a response and then Felinski heard him say 'Hauptbahnhof Hanover, bitte.' Then there was a pause before he spoke again: 'Herr Birkemeier, bitte – ja, von Leder hier. Guten Tag Herr Birkemeier, zuerst muss ich meine Grüsse geben – recht schönen Dank. Herr Direktor, ich erwartete einen passagier mit dem D-zug von Verlin – was ist die Situation im Moment?' And then with a sprinkling of 'Ach so's' and 'Ja's' and a few questions, von Leder talked for five minutes. When he had hung up, he turned and came back to his seat.

'It's the station at Hanover that got it. Part of it is still burning. The lines to Berlin are destroyed just east of Hanover and the train was stopped at Lehrte. It was very crowded and no transport was made available. Passengers had to fend for themselves.'

'Will you phone the station at Lehrte just to check that the phones are working. Your passenger could have telephoned you from there.'

The phones from Lehrte *were* still working and von Leder said, 'We'll take the small truck. You can lie low in the back.'

'When we get there I'll drop out and you get me called for. You can give a couple of others a lift and that'll give me really good cover.'

21

There was still quite a mob when they got to the level-crossing at Lehrte, and Felinski slid off the tail of the farm truck and walked into the crowd. A few minutes later he heard a voice from a loud-hailer shouting 'Baron von Leder sucht Herr Hartman.'

There were four others at the truck when Felinski got there and the introductions were laced with 'Merry Christmasses' and curses on the '*Terrorflieger*'. Now he'd have witnesses to his arrival and it was even better than the original cover.

Felinski kept to the cottage for the next two days and on the third day he was introduced to the farm staff. Back in London the farm records for the last five years had been carefully analysed and several plans for increasing its profitability had been worked out by agricultural experts. Felinski, as the new adviser to the von Leder farm and estate, had been thoroughly briefed on the plans and alternatives, and the thinking that made them practicable. Von Leder made clear to the farm staff that the new man would be spending much of his time at the schnapps plant in the Hanover suburbs.

Felinski set up the radio for the first time on the third night. The transmitter in the game-keeper's cottage was so isolated that if the Gestapo became suspicious it would be easy for direction-finding vans to pinpoint its location. All transmissions were to be of a maximum of five minutes. He had threaded a thin aerial wire up the massive oak beams to the crown of the open roof. London replied on schedule and briefly, and it seemed impossible that the Morse that came through the static was from the girl in the room on the top floor of Peter Robinson's.

By the end of the first week he had made two journeys to Hanover on the small motorbike and on both occasions he had spent time at the distillery and then gone to Schillerstrasse and looked up at the building with the green shutters.

On the eighth day, London had instructed him to start the operation.

The 3rd of January 1945 was bitter cold, and when Felinski arrived at the main Hanover railway station it was already dark and beginning to drizzle. Twice he was stopped for an identity check and when he got to the main hall he saw why.

The area was crowded with walking wounded and men on stretchers. There were at least three hundred men being attended to by doctors and nurses.

He walked slowly over towards them as if he were looking for someone and then stopped by a group standing huddled together, sharing two greatcoats between six of them. Two were Waffen SS and the others were Wehrmacht with Armoured Corps insignia. He stood near them and then moved over and asked if there was anyone from 2nd Panzer Division. Their faces were drawn and unshaven and they stood with the inertia of defeated men. They took cigarettes from him and he learned that they were part of the remnants of Hitler's push into the Ardennes.

The loudspeakers were relaying the news bulletin and an aggressive cheerful voice was announcing an all-out assault on Bastogne under Field-Marshal Model. The bread ration was to be reduced again immediately, and the words gave way to the strains of 'Ich Schenk mein Herz nur einem Mann . . .' In the gloom of the station the lovely voice seemed only to emphasize the doom-laden atmosphere. Felinski shivered as he walked to the notice-board with the messages pinned on from the bombed-out, refugees, and foreign workers. He had to look over it three times before he saw the card. It said 'Otto Hartman sucht seine Frau. Nachrichten erwartet', and there was a phoney telephone number which indicated that the card had been there for three days. The others were expecting him.

As he turned into Schillerstrasse the air-raid siren started its mournful wail and he looked up at the night sky. There were big clouds blowing across the moon and there was the sound of distant gunfire.

He stood opposite the house with the green shutters. The blackout covered all the windows but there was a small light which shone on a list of the occupants' names. On number seven was written 'Klement Vorster' in faded brown ink. He pressed the button and a few moments later there was a crackle and the loudspeaker said 'Ja'.

'Die Brücke ist kaput.'

There was a long pause and then a voice said slowly in German, 'What did you say?'

'The bridge is wrecked.'

The auto-lock buzzed and the door clicked open. There were

23

painted signs, with arrows and numbers painted black with red edges, pointing to the apartments. Number seven was on the second floor, up the concrete stairs. The man had not returned the password but Felinski guessed that they were not used to discipline of any kind. The door to number seven was ajar and there was a pink light coming from inside. He stood cautiously at the door, but nothing moved inside. There was no sound. From outside he could hear the noise of aircraft engines labouring under full load against the massive headwinds. He cautiously put his right hand forward to the open door, half expecting it to be flung wide open as his hand made contact. With a sickening jar he felt a gun thrust against his back. He heard the noise as the metal hit one of his ribs. Then a voice said quietly in German, 'Just walk in the room very quietly, very slowly.'

Felinski walked in carefully and as he heard the door close the gun jabbed his neck as the voice said, 'Turn round.'

The man was over six feet with corn-coloured hair in curls, like the statue of Michelangelo's 'David'. The face was pale and attractive in an ugly masculine way. The teeth looked perfect, clean and white as a bone. The eyes were cold and neither grey nor blue, neither pale nor dark, nondescript but compelling. The mouth was full, sensuous and dry. The gun was almost touching Felinski's nose, and he focused his eyes on the man's face as he said, 'The bridge is wrecked,' and the man said in Russian, 'Say it again.'

Felinski said nothing and then after a long silence the man said in German, 'And the water comes higher.'

Felinski smiled and spoke in Russian. 'Comrade Voronov, I must teach you how to hold a man with a gun. The way you do it is dangerous – to you.'

Voronov lowered the gun and waved Felinski to a chair. 'Why do they send you, comrade?'

'I have brought you a radio, money, documents and a letter from your mother. And I bring you help.'

Voronov laughed softly. 'What help can you give, gospodin?'

'You are a brave man, Voronov, I should like you to be acknowledged after this is all over. I can help you survive.'

The pale face flushed with anger. 'The bastards did not even answer my call sign.'

'There can be many reasons for that.'

'You don't know the reason then, comrade?'

'Where is the radio?'

'We'll talk about radios all in good time. When I am ready.'

'Fine. Now put that gun away and let's talk. Have you got anything I can transmit for you today?'

Voronov smiled and looked at him with half-closed eyes. 'You soon make yourself at home, comrade.' He shrugged. 'Maybe that's a good thing. You said you got papers for me. You got them here?'

Felinski opened his jacket and took out a small flat package wrapped in soft yellow oilskin and proffered it to Voronov. Voronov didn't reach for it. He said, 'OK, you open it friend.'

Felinski approved and noted the peasant caution, and carefully untied the knots and broke the small red wax seal. He pulled back the cloth and handed over the papers. Voronov sat down on the edge of the divan bed and Felinski looked around the room. The walls were bare and the room as a whole gave no hint of its owner's personality. There was a small Blaupunkt radio on a table, and curtained off from the room was what looked like a small kitchen. On the floor was linoleum except for a small rug near the divan. A handful of Tauchnitz pocket editions leaned sideways on a single shelf alongside a thick book that was upside down. Felinski read its title laboriously. It was *Vom Winde Verweht* and he wondered what Voronov made of Scarlett O'Hara and Rhett Butler.

As Voronov read the various items he put them beside him on the bed. It was nearly half an hour before he had finished and he tapped his finger on the pile. 'Your people are trying to help all right. You want to take over the group now you are here?'

'What do *you* want? You've done very well on your own.'

Voronov shook his head, 'Not really, it was just luck with the girl, otherwise I get nothing.'

'What training did you have?'

'Two months at Moscow Centre.'

'Where did you do your radio training?'

'At Sehjodnya.'

Felinski knew that this was the NKVD's radio training centre for low-grade agents. It was about 25 miles north-east of Moscow and its training was not good enough for an agent in enemy territory, especially in time of war. It was meant for line-crossers, and partisans operating on enemy lines of communication.

'What was the radio – an R07 maybe?'

Voronov grinned. 'You know too much comrade. Yes it was an R07.'

'Where is it now?'

'In a locker at the station.'

'How long has it been there?'

'Three months. I put it there when Moscow don't answer. Maybe it needs repair. I get it for you tomorrow.'

'No. Don't go near it. The Gestapo will be watching the locker by now. They examine lockers every two or three days. They'll have found it long ago and be waiting for someone to claim it. Forget it.'

Voronov looked up at Felinski, examining his face carefully, and then he said, 'You take over comrade, but I like to know one thing first.'

'What's that?'

'After the war what happens?'

Suddenly, because of the question, Felinski felt great warmth for the man. This was how you made a refugee. This was what Nansen passports were all about. Voronov may be tough, he may be brave, but when it was all over who would care about him? His suspicious countrymen had left him to rot. The British would do something, but it wouldn't be much.

'You'll be looked after Voronov. I shall see to that. You can come back to England with me, or we'll talk to Moscow if that's what you want.'

Voronov stood up and put out a big hand. 'My name is Kliment.'

'Mine is Stephen.'

And it was as simple as that. Felinski shared the divan and when the curfew was clear he left in the morning. They had arranged a 'place of conspiracy' for emergencies, Voronov had been given a code pad, and he was to arrange for Felinski to meet the girl the following afternoon, a Saturday. Back at the farm Felinski set up the radio and reported back to London that contact had been made.

.   .   .   .   .

They met at the Goethestrasse bridge that spanned the Leine, but Felinski saw that Voronov was alone.

'The girl wouldn't come. Said she didn't want to be seen with us in public.'

'Doesn't she go out with you in public?'

Voronov laughed. 'Yes, but that's different. She's in love with me.'

'Where will she meet me?'

'She's back at my room now. She'll see us there if you want.'

'OK, that's fine. Tell me about the others.'

'There's only two left now. Bering was killed in an air-raid three months ago. Mazurov and Rykov we could meet tomorrow.'

'What do they do? What's their cover?'

'We've all got good documents. The Fräulein fixed those. Rykov is a gardener at the castle and Mazurov works as a long-distance driver for a food company. I'm a cleaner at the Gauleitung.'

'What information do the others provide?'

'Rykov reports on troop trains, he can't do much more. Mazurov takes the stuff to Liège. We won't need him for that any more. Now you are here we can send it by radio.'

'What are they like?'

Voronov shrugged. 'They're both good men, good patriots, but not well trained.'

Back at the room in the Schillerstrasse Voronov tapped three times on the door and a key was turned and they went in. When he had closed the door Voronov said, 'Herr Hartman, this is Fräulein Lange.'

The girl was very young, in her early twenties. Tall and slim with long black hair. She wasn't merely pretty, she was beautiful. Her eyes were a clear grey, wide-set as if to balance the wide, soft mouth. She looked calmly at Felinski and then nodded and sat on the divan beside Voronov. Felinski took the wooden chair. The other two sat quietly, waiting for him to speak.

'Fräulein Lange, before we say anything else I must give you a message from my superiors. We think the war will be over inside the next six months – the war in Europe that is. When it is over you will be offered a sum of money sufficient for you to live on for the rest of your life. You will have every protection that may be necessary and any other help you ask for.'

Neither the girl nor Voronov spoke. He waited a few moments and then continued.

'Have you taken any precautions to check if you are under surveillance?'

Voronov shook his head. 'No. We are sure she is not being watched.'

Felinski nodded. 'I'll check myself in the next few days.'

The girl spoke and he was conscious of the soft voice and the big grey eyes looking at his face. 'I know too much about the Gauleiter for that to happen.'

'It's not just the Gauleiter, Fräulein Lange, there's an Abwehr Stelle here, a main Gestapo office, and three SD detachments.' He paused and then said, 'Apart from the professionals there are people who could be jealous merely because of your good looks.'

He saw Voronov nod his head vigorously and the girl dismissed them both. 'There are things to tell you. Urgent things. Today the Russians crossed the Oder. Zhukov's men. The Vi rockets are being concentrated from now on on Antwerpen. And Gauleiter Lauterbacher is making arrangements to leave if things get worse. He is leaving his wife and family here and taking one of the girls from the office with him.'

Felinski looked at the girl and thought that the Gauleiter must be mad not to take this young beauty with him. As if she were exactly reading his thoughts she said, 'The Gauleiter prefers blondes.'

Felinski smiled. 'How fortunate, but how stupid, Fräulein Lange.'

And for the first time she smiled. She was very bright but she was open to masculine flattery, and that must have served Voronov well.

Chapter 5

By the first week in March Felinski had brought the group to a well-organized unit with its members better trained, and with improved security. The girl was still supplying top-grade material and she was able to bring out selected material that London asked for. The rest of the group were now trained to cover identification of military units and their movements. Felinski had acted as sheepdog to check whether the girl was under surveillance and the results were negative. They were now a team and without formal declaration Felinski was accepted as the natural leader and Voronov had become an efficient deputy.

On the evening of 10 March Felinski had cycled to Hanover. Voronov had been sent to Holzminden with other workers to erect barbed-wire perimeter fences for a POW camp there, but the girl was bringing a copy of that day's situation report from the Gauleiter to Hitler's command post outside Berlin at Zossen.

Felinski slid the key quietly into the lock and turned it smoothly. He turned as he shut the door. There was a small light with a coloured shade by the divan and it shone its pink light romantically across the white sheets. The girl lay with her black hair spread across the pillow and her face was turned towards Felinski. She was naked, and the pink light made her look even more beautiful. Rykov's face was buried in the pillow by her shoulder as he lay between her legs. She made no move to stop Rykov but the big grey eyes looked calmly at Felinski as the Russian used her body. Felinski stood transfixed and then, as if sensing the tension, Rykov lifted his head and the girl said, 'Guten Abend, Herr Hartman.' Rykov turned quickly and, seeing Felinski, he seemed to be on his feet and pulling up his rough shapeless trousers all in one movement. He reached back to the end of the divan for his shirt, and when that was on he said, 'You want me any more, Herr Hartman?'

Felinski looked at the pale rough face, hesitated for a moment, and then said slowly, 'No, not tonight Rykov. There is work to be done and you cannot help.'

Rykov picked up his jacket from a chair. 'Shall you tell Kliment, Herr Hartman?'

Felinski shook his head slowly. 'No, I don't think that would help. Did you bring a report today?'

Rykov nodded. 'Yes, I covered the main station twice today.' And he pointed at an envelope on the table. Then he let himself out of the room. He said nothing to the girl.

The girl had lit a cigarette and was sitting on the divan, her back against the pillows and the wall. He looked at the calm, beautiful face and the big grey eyes looked calmly back, and inevitably his eyes went to the full breasts and their hard pink nipples. As his eyes went back to her face he saw the soft generous lips parted with a half-smile and she said softly, 'You like what you see, Herr Hartman?'

'You're very beautiful Fräulein Lange . . . but why Rykov?'

She shrugged slowly. 'He needed a woman.'

'And Voronov?'

'He gets all he wants.'

Felinski pulled up a chair and sat down.

'What are your feelings for Voronov?'

'I love him. I would die for him.'

'And Rykov?'

'A friend, one of us. He needs a woman sometimes. Better if it is me.'

'And you don't mind?'

She looked at him and slowly shook her head. She took a pull at her cigarette and turned to stub it in the ashtray on the floor. He watched the big firm breasts tremble with her movements and then she sat up again. 'No I don't mind,' and she looked at him without embarrassment. Their eyes seemed locked and the soft pink light seemed dim and then as he looked at her she said softly, 'You want me like that, Englishman, don't you.'

Felinski sat silent and tried to find an answer as his lust fought with his training. As he hesitated, the girl stretched out the long shapely legs, and he could see the black fleece between her thighs. She lay there looking at him, waiting for him to rational-

30

ize what she knew he would do, and finally she leant up on one elbow and said, 'Just tell me. Do you want me?'

Felinski nodded.

'Is it Voronov?'

'Yes. I don't want to hurt him.'

She spoke quickly. 'He will not know. He will have me when he is here. But tonight you can love me.'

'What about you?'

She smiled. 'I like you to do it to me, Englishman,' and as he stood up she held out her arms.

His months of abstinence and the excitement of the girl's body were so much that he was only conscious of her arms around him and her body responding eagerly to his as his lust overwhelmed him. He rationalized the first time but could find no excuse for the lust that made him have her again and again. When it was over the girl had made it easy for them both. She had handed over the Gauleiter's reports. They included the confirmation that the US Ninth Armoured Division had crossed the Rhine at Remagen on 7 March and that eight of the defending Wehrmacht commanders had been executed on Hitler's personal orders.

When he was ready to go the girl had put her hand on his arm and said, 'Do you like me, Englishman?' and she looked as though it mattered.

Felinski smiled at her and kissed the full soft lips. 'Yes. I like you. More than like you.'

As he turned to the door she said softly, 'Englishman, you don't even know my name.'

He turned quickly and he saw there were tears in the big grey eyes. 'I'm sorry. I really am. Tell me, please.'

'Lise – Lise Maria.'

As Felinski cycled back in the darkness his mind was full of conflicting emotions and attitudes. One layer of his thoughts was shame at using the girl who was already risking her life because of her love for another man. The indecency of the abuse of her willingness and Voronov's courage and loyalty seemed enormous. But his mind would not forgo the erotic memories of the girl and what she had let him do. And looming behind it all was the possible effect it would have on the group. He knew that what he had done was unforgivable in terms of intelligence work. To become emotionally involved in any way with the principal source of top-grade information was asking for big trouble. And to enjoy sexually the close girlfriend of his deputy was inviting disaster. He fleetingly wondered what Franks's reaction would be if he knew. He'd have him drummed out of the Intelligence Corps for a start.

It was nearly four in the morning when he completed the transmission and put the radio back under the grating.

In the next ten days he was heavily loaded with radio transmissions. Voronov was back and seemed in good spirits. He had seen Rykov twice and he had been his normal impassive self. Mazurov had been injured during an air-raid and had sick-leave from his work for ten days. Voronov and Felinski were using him as a watcher.

In the last week of March it was clear that the machinery of government in Germany was grinding to a halt. Hanover was thronged with refugees from the Rhine, where Montgomery and Simpson were smashing Model's Army Group B. The radio programmes were constantly broken into by announcements of new and contradictory edicts from Berlin. And the ration cards were no longer honoured. The food wasn't there any more.

On the last day of March Felinski had heard the bombers as they turned with their loads to Hanover, Hildesheim and Brunswick. It wasn't even dark yet but there seemed to be no defence for the towns, and the distant crunch of bombs was sickening. Felinski's thoughts went to Voronov and the girl. He hadn't seen her for over three weeks and he hurried to the shed for the old bicycle, and headed off in the direction of Hanover. This time he took the main road. It was three miles shorter than the lanes. Only two miles from the town he met the first of the refugees. It seemed, even now, impossible that there were German refugees. Carts and prams, horse-drawn wagons and even donkeys with double loads, and hundreds of silent women and children. Many were exhausted and sat by the ditches, and some were covered in blood-stained bandages. Their faces were closed and bruised in the sudden knowledge of defeat. There were Wehrmacht men in tattered field-grey with their insignia and rank badges torn off. As so often on days of war and tragedy, the sun shone from a pale blue sky and the fleecy clouds of spring were almost motionless. Up where the blue was darker, there were contrails from four aircraft that were circling lazily without any opposition.

He spoke to one of the men and asked him what it was like in Hanover, and he said he didn't know, but he moved his arm in a wide sweeping arc and added 'Hildesheim kaput.' An old woman with tears pouring down her face said 'No more Hanover, it's gone, it's flat' and as she brushed the back of her hand to her eyes the crowds were running to the ditches, flattening themselves and their children to the ground. He heard the shouts of 'Schpitfeur! Terrorflieger.' And there they were, two beautiful Spitfires coming down out of the sun, and he wanted to shout to the cowering people that these were RAF, they didn't shoot unarmed refugees. And as his mouth made no noise the two planes opened fire on the narrow road and sprayed it with cannon and machine-gun bullets. They zoomed off west towards Hanover and nobody tried to help the injured and the dying. There was no help to give.

It was nearly four hours before Felinski got to the outskirts of Hanover and the whole town seemed on fire. He chained his cycle to a set of twisted iron railings. It would be useless in the city.

A pall of smoke hung over the town and there was the red glow of fires reflected from the underside. Every few minutes something would explode, and the dark red would become bright orange for a few moments, and then settle back to the sulky red of the burning buildings. The roads had gone, they were covered with the debris of houses, not just a scattering of bricks but ten feet high banks of rubble. He could hear people shouting and crying and even as he watched, the wall of a big house fell silently forward and slowly exploded into bricks and concrete as it hit the ground. Debris rained down near him and he moved off following a line of bent street lights. It was dawn when he got to the Schillerstrasse and he was exhausted by the effort of the nightmare journey. In the early morning light he could see that the house front looked intact, and he struggled over great heaps of debris and then stood looking at the ruins. The first rays of a pale sun lit the back of the house. Each floor sagged down to touch the ground as if it had melted. Only the

33

front still stood, the rest had gone. The bodies in the heaps of rubble would stay until they rotted. There was no authority left, no government for the defeated Germans of Hanover.

It was midday before he found the road back to the farm and now he walked. It was impossible to find one's way about the city any more. There were too few recognizable places and only the river still kept to its old line.

The tide of refugees had turned south and there were only small groups now, lining the ditches and preparing to sleep out for the night. It was late afternoon when he got back to the cottage in the woods. He had a long radio contact with London and was ordered to stop the operation until he received further instructions. He gave full details of what he had seen on the roads and in Hanover, and he informed them that all his team were missing, almost certainly killed in the air-raid.

Work on the farm had been abandoned and the men were armed with shotguns to warn off intruders. A Red Cross Station had been opened at the big house and loaves of bread were given to refugees with children.

It was late in the afternoon, almost a week later, when there was a knock on the cottage door. Felinski was lying on the bed. He sat up carefully and reached under the bed for his gun. He pushed the safety catch up and moved in his stockinged feet to the side of the door. He waited, but he could hear nothing except the creaking of the big trees. Then the knock came again and he called out 'Yes, who is it?' There was no reply and Felinski reached for the catch, slightly adjusted his grip on the gun, curled his finger to the trigger, and then flung open the wooden door. The girl was standing there. Her clothes were torn and muddy, her hair dishevelled, and at her feet was a straw case bound with a leather strap.

'My God Lise, come in.'

She seemed petrified, motionless, and he moved to her and gently guided her into the cottage. He sat her by the fire in the big comfortable chair and went outside for her case.

Her face was yellow with bruises and both her arms were covered in jagged cuts and she held her head back with her mouth open. He lifted her and carried her to the bed, and for an hour he gently washed her face, her legs and her arms. She slept through it all and as he waited he opened her case. There was a sweater and skirt, some needles and thread. There was a prayer book with a white vellum cover and a crucifix in gold. Inside, in ink, was written 'An unsere liebe Lise Maria, von Vati und Mutti, 20 April 1934. Erich von Lange, Schloss Einbeck, Nieder-Sachsen.' So the lovely girl was an aristocrat from a castle. And she'd been confirmed on Hitler's birthday in 1934. There was a fine gold bracelet with an eagle crest and three keys on a ring. There was a short length of bloodstained bandage and a creased photograph of a small girl sitting with a man and a woman on the stone steps of a large ornate mansion.

And now she was lying bruised and exhausted in a farm cottage. She'd done more than most soldiers to win the war. All she had to do was stay alive, and she'd get money and a medal, but she'd have to live outside Germany for the rest of her life.

The girl was still sleeping at midnight when von Leder called at the cottage. He looked at the girl and then turned to Felinski.

'The house is packed with refugees from the east and they're full of tales of Russian troops raping and killing as they go. Have you any news at all? Is it possible the Russians will get this far?'

Felinski shook his head. 'No, there's no chance of that. The Americans will be here in the next few days. London have told me that officially. I am responsible for your safety and if you were in danger from the Russians I would let you know. Just hang on – that's all we've got to do.'

'And if London are wrong?'

'Then I shall call up a helicopter for you.'

'And what about you?'

'My orders are to wait for the Americans.'

'Why don't they lift you out now?'

'It's not necessary. There's too much fighting going on. I can wait.'

Von Leder looked at the girl.

'I've seen her somewhere, is she local?'

'No she's not.'

Von Leder looked at Felinski and smiled faintly. 'OK. You keep your secrets.' Then at the door he turned, looking tired and dispirited. 'I can't get out of my mind what is going to happen to us Germans now. Especially those at the mercy of the Russians.'

'They'll need men like you to speak for them.'

Von Leder looked at him intently. 'Your words will count more than mine. And what will you say when they say it all over again – "The only good German is a dead one"?'

Felinski's grey eyes were unblinking as he looked at von Leder. And he said quietly, 'Herr Baron, there's no use pretending. There won't be any mercy for a long long time to come. All we can hope for is that when the fighting is over, justice is a good enough substitute for mercy. Justice is the best that your people can hope for.'

'So people like me have wasted their efforts.'

'No. Never. It's people like you who will have made the justice possible. Otherwise there would just have been revenge.'

There were tears on von Leder's cheeks.

'Goodnight.'

'Goodnight, Herr Baron.'

At 1.15 p.m. that day, Central Time, a woman was painting a portrait of a man in a dark grey suit and a red Harvard tie. The man put his hand to his head and closed his eyes. At 3.35 p.m. he was dead. That was at Warm Springs, Georgia, and it was 4.50 p.m. Washington Time before Mrs Roosevelt was told.

At the same time the representative of the International Committee of the Red Cross had reached Oranienburg, 19 miles north of Berlin. He stood with tears pouring down his face as a man screamed at him in frenzied rage. The man was SS-Standartenführer Keindel and his voice was only just audible over Zhukov's guns that were pounding and roaring ten miles east of Berlin. Forty thousand souls sat, lay, knelt, and crumpled, as the SS man roared his contempt and refusal to turn his prisoners over to the protection of the Red Cross. He was the commander of Sachsenhausen.

At almost the same time, at Klossen, a small town on the east bank of the Elbe, a single oil-splattered Russian tank, a T-34, stood in the main square. There were eight Russians with black tank-corps helmets. On the cobblestones, which shone with rain, was the glass from broken bottles. They had a young German woman against the side of the tank and two small children clung to her skirts. There was a group of nine or ten elderly civilians who stood watching silently. The girl's head was pressed back as they thrust a bottle to her mouth. Most of them were drunk but they still carried their guns. Against their shouts could be heard the children's screams and then a sergeant lifted one of them like a bundle of rags and smashed it against the tracks of the tank. The others laughed as he killed the baby the same way. Then the girl was shoved to the floor and they took turns in raping her while the small crowd watched, paralysed.

All over Germany the birds were flying home to roost.

The girl awoke just after dawn. The rain was beating down outside and as she moved to sit up she closed her eyes and lay back on the pillow. He sat on the edge of the bed and looked at the bruised face. After a few moments he said gently, 'How do you feel?' She moved her head slightly and a few moments later he could tell from her breathing that she was asleep.

Felinski listened to the BBC news at midday and he heard that Field-Marshal Model was now surrounded and cut off in the Ruhr. It couldn't be long now. But it was.

Felinski slept on rugs in front of the fire and when he woke the girl was sitting up in bed looking at him as she smoked a cigarette. He stood up and walked over to her.

'How do you feel?'

'Much, much better.'

'What news of Voronov?'

She shook her head. 'No news. I went to the house, it was destroyed.'

'How much destroyed?'

'Only the front wall was standing.'

'What happened to you?'

'I went to the station and there was an explosion. I was unconscious. When I came to I came here, it took a long time.'

'How did you know about this place?'

'Voronov told me.'

'How did he know?'

'He had you followed.'

'Who did the following?'

'A local party man.'

'You mean a KPD man?'

She nodded. 'Yes, he sometimes gave Voronov money when he was first here.'

The man sounded safe enough. Voronov had obviously absorbed his training even if he hadn't absorbed the discipline.

'What do you think happened to Voronov?'

'I think he is dead.'

Felinski looked at her. He could see no trace of her feelings on her bruised face as she returned his stare.

She ate soup and potatoes and drank a glass of milk while he told her what was happening in the world outside.

An hour later he stood outside the door of the cottage with the girl. There was an early morning mist that shrouded the tops of the trees and rolled between their heavy lower branches. Birds sang, and all the world seemed deathly silent. There were no sounds except the sounds of the wood and its natural inhabitants. After a few moments the girl shivered and he led her back inside to the fire. As they sat there she said, 'It's all so peculiar. In here it's peaceful and warm, and there's enough to eat. But outside thousands of people are killing one another.' She looked at him. 'It's sickening.'

'I'll look after you.'

'I wasn't thinking about me.' And she put her face in her hands and sobbed.

'Is it Voronov?'

She looked up at him her face wet with tears, and she nodded. 'It's Voronov and all the world. We're all mad animals.'

Chapter 6

Like an oasis in time they spent the next five days peacefully. It seemed safe to walk in the woods and the days were sunny and warm for April. Felinski kept contact with London and at the girl's wish he made love to her fiercely and often. But they were eating when the door was kicked open and the two soldiers came in.

Both were tall and young. Wearing torn and dirty uniforms. Both carried Thompson sub-machine guns. The one with sergeant's stripes had looked at them both, vaguely waving the gun in their direction.

The corporal said, 'Look at the dame, sarge. She sure is stacked.'

The sergeant was chewing gum and he said 'Aus' as he waved his gun towards the door, but his eyes were on the girl's sweater. 'Aus,' he said again.

Felinski didn't stand up. He didn't look towards the soldiers as he said in English, 'I don't know who you two are, but whoever you are, I want you to inform your commanding officer that I should like to meet him and talk to him.' He wiped a piece of bread in the last remnants of bacon fat on his plate, and only then did he stand up. He walked over to the sergeant, who raised his gun to Felinski's chest and pushed the barrel against him. The shifty eyes held Felinski's stare and they only blinked when the corporal said, 'Don't trust him, sarge. He's a Kraut, like those bastards in the Ardennes. Remember? I'll take him out and you entertain the dame, and I'll come back for my turn.'

The sergeant hesitated and then he said to Felinski, 'Put your hands up pig-face. High.'

There was only a small rattle as Felinski's hands came up but he was standing with the gun in both hands and it was pointing at the corporal and nothing seemed to have happened. There'd been no struggle but the gun had changed hands. His finger checked the safety catch. The corporal made a clumsy movement and Felinski fired three shots. Not a burst but three shots. The first hit the corporal's hand and the second knocked the gun from his hands. The third thunked into the door. Felinski told the girl to hand him the fallen gun. He tucked it under his left arm, reached for the magazine catch and jerked down the drum magazine. He shook it. It was part loaded and he wound the key and smiled when he heard the mainspring break. He handed it to the sergeant and said, 'Never poke guns at strangers, sergeant. They don't all like it.' He turned to the girl and said, 'Lise, you take this gun. You're going to lock the door behind me. The safety catch is off. If anybody comes through that door shoot 'em first and we'll sort it out later. When I come back I'll shout.'

And he'd waved the two out of the door and waited till he heard the lock turn in the door. They walked towards the big house and when they got to the big stone steps he said, 'Right, sergeant. You go in and tell your officer that I'm waiting to talk to him. Then you'd better get your corporal's hand fixed.'

A couple of minutes later an officer walked out. He had grey crew-cut hair and wore a lieutenant-colonel's star. Felinski saluted and said, 'Major Felinski, sir. British Army on special duties. My identity documents, sir.' The military formality seemed to impress the colonel and he looked carefully through the papers. He checked Felinski's face against the photograph. Then he handed back the papers, and hands on hips he nodded to Felinski. 'OK, Major. You'll have to go to G2. You need to eat before we take you?'

'No, sir, that's not necessary, but I have a collaborator with me, a German girl, and she must go too. And I must ask you to make special arrangements for Baron von Leder in the house.'

The colonel nodded slowly, the pale-blue eyes looking at Felinski with the beginning of respect. 'I'd been warned about him from Div. And I think I've heard about you too. Were you dropped by parachute?'

'Yes.'

The tough face was suddenly friendly and a big hand grasped Felinski's. 'Look. Why don't you get the girl and we'll celebrate.'

Felinski smiled. 'Thanks Colonel, but I can't draw any attention to the girl. And I think you ought to treat von Leder as if he is being arrested. At least in front of his family and staff.'

40

'That's fine, Major. That's just what I've done. He's on his way to G2. In a truck. I'm taking over this place as my head-quarters so I shall be able to keep an eye on them all. Now what do you want to do?'

'Where is the nearest British unit?'

'I don't really know. Let me check.'

The colonel gave them his requisitioned Mercedes and his driver. They went back to the cottage and he put together their belongings. The girl had her straw case. Felinski had one bag and his transmitter. He glanced around to check that there was nothing left, and with no regrets he closed and locked the door.

They were at 30 Corps headquarters late that evening, and in London by noon the next day. A smiling Franks had met them at the airfield at Tempsford.

The day they finished de-briefing him he was looking out of one of the windows across Whitehall and as he idly looked he saw a Spitfire doing victory rolls in the cloudless blue sky. The pilot was making a very good guess. The next day was VE day.

Franks in civilian clothes seemed to lose none of his authority as he leaned forward with his arms on the table. His right hand was idly rolling a pencil from side to side on a blotter. He was looking intently at Felinski.

'Your pay in SIS would be tax free, Stephen, and that's worth quite a bit.'

'Yes, I know.'

'You'd have the choice of France or Germany.'

Felinski shook his head. 'I really mean it. I've made up my mind. I've had enough. For now anyway. The war in Europe's over and I'd like to be a civilian again. Maybe you would allow me to contact you again later on.'

'Certainly. We shall probably keep in touch with you anyway. Any idea what you're going to do?'

'No. I'll have to look around and see what's going. What's happening to the girl?'

Franks looked up and across at Felinski, hesitated for a moment, as if treading carefully, and then said, 'If you're interested in her emotionally Steve, I'll put you in touch with her right away. If it's only physical I think you'd do her a good turn if you forgot her. She's got enough to cope with at the moment.'

'I just want to know that she's being cared for and that she's got some plan for the future.'

Franks nodded. 'Fine. You're entitled to know. Financially she's all right. She's getting a lump sum and a pension. She's going to be given British nationality and she's deciding now whether to go to Spain or Canada. I think it'll be Spain. Emotionally she's a mess. Time will sort it out but we're trying to take a few short cuts. I think if she can be kept away from anything to do with the war she'll settle back quickly. She was fond of you – and of Voronov for that matter. She really needs to be with people who will just know her as a pretty girl. People who were not deeply involved in the war.'

'And what about von Leder?'

Franks leaned back and fiddled with the pencil again. He pursed his lips before he spoke. 'Now that's a real mess if you like. Totally disillusioned. The farm's like a fortress. Refused any reward or help and goes out of his way to defy any Milgov laws that he doesn't like. We'd be glad to let him get away with it except that he's an influential figure and everybody takes their time from him.'

'Could I help?'

Franks looked up and smiled as he shook his head slowly. ''Fraid not Steve. We did make a gentle suggestion on those lines. Said he'd shoot you if he found you on his land.'

'Regrets helping us?'

'It's hard to say. No, I don't think it's really that. More a desperate frustration that the risks he took don't seem to have helped his countrymen. Considers himself a traitor. If it wasn't for that huge family of his he'd make it known.'

'What's to be done for him?'

'Nothing much. Just head him off from doing anything really silly and hope he settles down.'

If, in the postwar years, you had an income from a two thousand acre farm, you didn't really need to work. Not even if only half the income was yours.

Large organizations had looked at the tough young man who came to their interviews. They liked the DSO, but they didn't like the private income. And somehow they couldn't categorize the man who had been to Harrow and Christ Church, whose English was better than theirs, yet went with a name like Felinski. Although the Polish origins went back a hundred years they found it disturbing. Some were interested enough to ask where Poland was.

Gradually the ties of family and friends slipped away. The man who had come back seemed too cold, too self-sufficient. There seemed to be a deliberate absence of conventional response. It was the behaviour of a man being calm in the eye of a storm. It was the appearance of a man in unfriendly country, whose face was closed in order to give nothing away.

There were some years growing pyrethrum in Kenya, and after 'Uhuru' there were two years as a white hunter. On a three-month leave in England Felinski had planned a week in Rye. He'd seen the 'For Sale by Auction' notice outside the farm on the last day. The auction was the following week and the bidding had been brisk. Felinski hadn't come in till it hung at £30,000. At £32,000 the locals gave up and it was his. He didn't appear to be listening, he just nodded, and they had guessed he was going to have it whatever it cost. They ran it up another £500 just for devilment, and then left him to it. Another city slicker who'd pour money into a middling farm. They rather liked them. They'd seen 'em come, and they'd seen 'em go. They'd buy it in a couple of years when he ran out of money. They'd done it before. With a couple of new barns and brand-new machinery provided by the sucker, they'd decide who'd have it and buy it for less than the new boy had paid. Romney Marsh sheep are bred for survival and Romney Marsh farmers are much the same.

PART TWO

Chapter 7

It was that bit of October that farmers call 'St Luke's little summer' because it's frequently a little summer all on its own. And St Luke or not, it was raining cats and dogs. The flat landscape of the Romney Marshes is not renowned for its beauty even when the sun shines, and in the rain it looked desolate and uninviting. The sky was an even, dull, grey and in the west it was black and ominous. There were sheets of standing water on the flat fields where the mole drains couldn't carry the water away, and a small car had driven into the ten-acre field so that its occupants, late season trippers, could eat their sandwich lunch. As Felinski watched them and saw the deep ruts that the car wheels had cut in the field, he turned to the man sitting at the pine table. 'I suppose town people will never, never, realize that grass is a crop.'

The man smiled as he looked up. 'These year-end figures are good, Steve, whichever way you look at them.'

'Depends on how you look at them.'

'You make a profit on everything, Steve – sheep, poultry, fruit, seed and potatoes. Above-average profits too.'

'Oh, sure we do.'

'Well what're you grumbling at?'

'Was I grumbling?'

The other man laughed. 'No, but you were standing around as if you wanted to.'

Felinski smiled. 'You're a shrewd bastard, young Mason, just like your old man.'

'Look. You're making a good profit however you look at it – profit per acre or profit on money invested. You're probably the only farmer in this area without an overdraft at the bank.' He turned to his papers and then looked over to Felinski. 'Steve, you've got forty thousand in the bank or invested elsewhere. The farm is worth about three hundred thousand not counting stock. You made ten thousand plus this last year. So what's it all about?'

Felinski sighed and sat down at the table. 'I guess I'm bored.'

'You know what you need?'

'What?'

'A woman.'

'I've got a woman, for God's sake.'

'Lavender?'

'Yes.'

'Well, why don't you marry her? She's the prettiest thing for miles around. She'll make a good wife and she worships you.'

Felinski shook his head. 'I'm too much a loner to be married. Anyway I'm over fifty and she's twenty-two.'

'Oh for heaven's sake. You're healthier and tougher than most men half your age. Anyway she wouldn't give a damn about that.'

Felinski reached for the accounts. 'She's a good kid,' he said, to dismiss the subject. But Mason ignored the reaching hand and, looking intently at Felinski, he said, 'Don't you find her attractive, Steve?'

Felinski laughed, startled. 'Of course I do. She's an absolute doll. So what?'

Mason plucked up his courage visibly and said, 'Well, if you don't want to marry her, at least you can sleep with her. Do you both good.'

Felinski jerked up his head, red-faced with indignation. 'Well I'm damned. Here you are, a respected and respectable accountant suggesting I sleep with a girl half my age instead of marrying her. She's the vicar's daughter for God's sake.'

Mason persisted. 'Somebody's going to screw her if you don't. She's the parson's daughter, not the parson; and half the county's sniffing round her. And there ain't any doubt in my mind, she'd rather have you.'

'Let's talk about the access roads.'

'OK. Talk.'

'We've got seven tons of chicken muck to get out of the battery houses every week and Foreman's lorry takes twice as long as it should filling up the silos. They haven't complained yet. But they will.'

'How much will it cost?'

'Even if we do it ourselves it'll be a thousand. It's got to take a twenty-ton tanker.'

48

'Look Steve, you work this farm very economically. There's only Bill Weeks and yourself, and Mrs Weeks on the eggs. Anything you can do to make life easier is a good buy. I'd get a contractor to do it. It's worth the extra.'

'Fair enough. Now let's review those damned share portfolios.'

And they'd talked for another hour before they went to the Red Lion at Appledore for lunch.

The rain persisted until mid-afternoon and Felinski had signed cheques and made various telephone calls. He was standing by the window listening to the ringing tone and looking out at the farm buildings. The small farmhouse had been built about 1450 but it had been kept in good repair. It was well furnished and had a friendly, warm atmosphere despite its solitary owner. Across the yard was an oast that held the repair shop and spares, and alongside was a good barn used for lambing and storage. There were two good white-washed stables and he could see Bill Weeks leading out the chestnut mare. The man bent to feel the mare's lower leg where it had been cut by barbed wire the week before at the Ashford Hunt. Then Weeks stood up, and as he straightened he waved at someone. It was the girl. She pushed her cycle up the slope of the yard and leaned it against the stables. She stood talking to Weeks for a few moments and then bent down to feel the mare's leg. The mare put down her head and nuzzled the long blonde hair. The girl stood up laughing and shook her hair, said something to Weeks who pointed to the house, and the girl walked across the yard. He had known her since she was fourteen, and even then Lavender Coombs had been a beauty. And now there was a generous, intelligent mind and an outgoing personality to enhance the pretty face and the shapely body. As she came past the window she saw him and waved. As usual she let herself in.

'Hi fatso. The mare looks good again.'

He put down the phone and turned to her. 'Hi skinny. You look good yourself.'

She sat herself comfortably in one of the big armchairs.

'And to what do I owe this visit?'

'Oh,' she said. 'Your magnetic charm and a message from Mother. Wants to know if you'll eat with us tonight.'

49

'Somebody dropped out?'

'No, you bastard, my mother doesn't do things like that and well you know it. She thinks the lonely bachelor might need a change from eating his own poached eggs.'

'I'll make us a cuppa.'

As he was stirring the mugs of tea in the kitchen he called out to her 'Lav – you like to go to the flicks after we've eaten?'

'Don't *call* me that, you pig. What flicks – where?'

'Tunbridge Wells.'

'Ho, ho. The big city itself. What's on?'

'It's *Dr Zhivago*.'

'Again?'

'Again.'

He came in carrying the steaming mugs and she was smiling. She said, 'That would be lovely, Steve. You remember when we saw it before?'

He nodded. 'This is yours – full of fattening sugar.'

'Dad's stuck on his sermon. Looking to you for help.'

'Me?'

'Yes. He says you'd make a good parson. It's that closed-in face of yours. Listening to all the lies and saying nothing. Weighing us all up and finding us wanting.'

He looked across at her and said nothing.

She said, 'You're doing it now, you louse.'

'Actually I was thinking how gorgeous you are.'

'That's just turning the other cheek.'

He smiled at her. Sitting casually in the armchair, her long legs in the tight, faded blue jeans stretched out invitingly open as she smiled back at him. The blue eyes were an extraordinary blue, the sharp blue of cornflowers, and her mouth was wide and generous and her full top lip never quite covered the two front teeth. As a gesture to her father she seldom went bra-less, but her sweater was two sizes too small and only emphasized the thrust of her breasts. She was smiling as she spoke.

'Fatso, you're not supposed to stare at ladies' boobs like that. A quick look's OK, but not guessing the weight like at church bazaars.'

'You're wrong, honey. I was looking at your legs.'

'Which do you prefer?'

'What do you mean?'

50

'Which turns you on – my boobs or my legs?' He put his hands on his knees as if he were going to stand up. 'You really want to know, Miss Coombs, what turns me on?' She nodded.

He said slowly, 'I've often given it serious thought but I still can't make up my mind. Most of the time it's either your eyes or your mouth. They take turns at the head of the list.'

'You said "most of the time".'

'Ah yes. Well *all* of the time what turns me on is your honesty.'

And he stood up and picked up the mugs and walked into the kitchen.

She'd gone by the time he went back into the sitting-room.

Felinski swung the white MGC out of Tenterden's long High Street and took the Wittersham road. With less than two inches clearance under the exhaust he took all the humpbacked bridges slowly. As he turned into the farm gate he heard Max, his German Shepherd, barking a noisy welcome. When he had parked the car in the barn he walked across to the four big laying houses. The birds were on a long-day laying pattern and the lights were still on. There were four thousand birds in each house and there was the busy contented noise of feeding hens. He walked slowly down the gangways. They were used to him, and the brisk pecking heads couldn't spare him a glance. In most of the roll-downs there were two or three eggs, and they were mainly large and standards. There was no doubt that a good stockman like Weeks made all the difference. There was a nipple drinker not working, with a bird pecking at it angrily, and Felinski lifted his arm and eased the pipe. Probably an air lock. The water ran again and the bird pecked at the blob of water forming on the nipple. Everywhere was spotless and disinfected, the fans keeping the air sweet and clean. He checked all the doors and then walked slowly to the house.

The sky was clear now, with a big golden October moon. Across the fields he could see the pale blobs of the sheep. The lambs he'd kept back were bigger now than their dams.

Max was still barking and Felinski laughed sharply as the dog growled as he went in. He gave him fresh water and patted him roughly to calm him down, and closed the kitchen door as he walked into the sitting-room. He guessed it must be nearly midnight and he had to be up at six. But it had been a good evening and he was in the mood for a last whisky and some music. He walked over to the hi-fi and switched on the light. He chose the Schubert Trio, Opus 99, and as the arm came down to the disc he waited and listened. When the 'cello took over he turned and walked to the small oak corner cupboard. He was actually pouring the whisky when he saw the man sitting in the chair by the fire. He put the glass down slowly and then the decanter. But he didn't take his eyes off the man.

'OK. You've had your fun. Who are you?'

'Major Felinski?'

'I'm Felinski. Who are you?'

'My name's Maxwell, I'm with the CIA, and Franks advised me to talk to you. Colonel Franks, that is.'

'Why didn't you come in the normal way?'

'Partly because I didn't want anyone to know.'

'And partly what else?'

Maxwell grinned. 'Partly to see your reaction.'

Felinski didn't look amused. 'What is it you want?'

'Your help and advice.'

Felinski said nothing, but turned and poured himself a whisky. As he turned round Maxwell said, 'It may seem rude to say it in your house but it would make things easier if you sat down so that we could talk.'

Felinski leaned against the wall and looked at Maxwell. He was a medium-sized man, compactly built with good shoulders. His face was tanned and his hair crew-cut. The fingers spread out on each knee were stubby but well manicured. He had a white shirt and a polka-dot bow tie. His suit was a conservative grey tweed and his black shoes shone brightly. A vague bell rang at the back of Felinski's mind but he pushed it aside and twirled his whisky in the glass, tossed it down and put down the glass carefully. Then without moving he said quietly, 'Get out.'

Maxwell looked disbelieving. 'But this is important.' Then, as he looked at the frigid face and the unblinking eyes, with a sigh he stood up.

Felinski pointed. 'There's the door.'

Maxwell let himself out, and only when the door had closed behind him did Felinski move. He opened the kitchen door and gave the dog the freedom of the house.

He was asleep about fifteen minutes later.

Chapter 8

He was shaving and listening to the BBC's early morning farming programme when the phone rang.

'Lakers Farm.'

'Morning Stephen. Franks here. I gather you had a visitor last night.'

'True.'

'I gather he got a cold reception. Can I come and see you?'

'Of course.'

'Say in twenty minutes?'

'You'll take longer than that. About two and a half hours.'

'I'm at Rye, Steve. I motored down early this morning. I've booked in at the Mermaid.'

'Was all this because of last night?'

'I'd like to see you again, Steve. It's been a long time.'

Franks looked balder but not older; his hand-clasp was warm and his smile genuine. They sat down beside the blazing log fire. Felinski looked at his watch.

'My farm help will be here at eight. I'll have to break off for a few minutes to give them some changes if I'm not going to be around this morning.'

'That's fine Steve. Whatever is convenient for you.'

'Who is Maxwell anyway?'

Franks smiled and crossed his legs, making a slight, almost dismissive, waving gesture with his cigarette.

'Before we talk about him, let me go back a bit. Quite a long way really. Do you remember Voronov who was in your gang in Hanover?'

'Sure. He died in that bad raid, end of March, or beginning of April.'

Franks shook his head. 'He didn't actually. He didn't die, that is. He wasn't in Hanover when it was raided.'

'Where was he?'

'Well he decided that his relationship with you – us – could be

53

dangerous. Wasn't sure what his former masters in Moscow would make of it all. They were very trigger-happy at the time, as you know – still are for that matter. He actually left for Berlin just before the raid started that night on Hanover. Took him days to get there and, in fact, our friends got there before him. He reported to the NKVD HQ in Berlin and they shuffled him back to Moscow pretty sharpish. They did the usual thing – stuffed him in a cell at the Lubyanka and some months later got around to questioning him. Seems like they came to the conclusion that Voronov was a bit of a hero after all and he was sent to the Frunze Academy. Got the full treatment. Then he did a long stint of work and training with the MVD and finally was their Rezident in East Berlin. For the KGB, that is.'

There was a knock on the kitchen door and Felinski left the room. Franks looked around. It was a completely masculine room. Not uncomfortable but too tidy, too formal. There wasn't a picture, an ornament, or anything that gave a clue to the owner's personality. And maybe, Franks thought, that *was* the clue. When Felinski came back he brought coffee in mugs on a tray. The cheap metal tray was decorated with rather tasteless florid roses. And this was a very wealthy man, thought Franks.

'Does that surprise you, Steve?'

'I'm surprised that he didn't die in the raid and I'm a bit surprised that he did a bolt. The rest isn't surprising. The Moscow Centre had people coming back from all over after the war. They're heavy-handed enough at the best of times. With good training he'd be a first-class operator. What happened to the girl?'

Franks smiled. 'Ah yes, the girl. She carried a bit of a torch for you, Steve. At one time I wondered if it wasn't reciprocated. Anyway, we fixed her up. Let things die down a bit. She went over to Canada. Got a nice boutique there now. Married an Irishman. Got a couple of kids too.'

Felinski found himself thinking of the white naked body on the bed and Rykov . . . He shook his head, and noticing Franks's surprise he said, 'Sorry, I was thinking of something.'

'Ah, yes. Now the thing is, Voronov did a bolt again, three months ago. Surfaced in West Berlin and contacted one of the top CIA men there. They treated him well but were very cautious in case he was a plant. But what he spilled was the real

54

stuff. No doubt about it, and they finally decided to use him. He's now an important man in an unusually important operation, and that's where you come in.' He looked across at Felinski but the face was deadpan and the eyes were still. He went on. 'This is a joint operation between us – SIS, and the CIA. Maxwell is in charge of the CIA end of it. He's one of their really senior men. Very experienced.' He paused, but there was no response. 'The fact is Voronov has got the wind up. Thinks Maxwell doesn't know his stuff. That's why Maxwell came to see you.'

'I don't see how I can help him. It's his problem.'

'Well, both he and I want to make it yours, Steve. Not only us but other more important people.'

'Such as?'

'Such as the PM.'

Felinski frowned, 'You mean the Prime Minister?'

'Yes.'

Felinski banged both hands on the arms of the chair and stood up.

'The Prime Minister's never heard of me, for God's sake.'

'He has now.'

'Because a CIA "spook" can't handle a Russian defector?'

'No. Not that.'

'What then?'

'Because he wants Leggat back.'

'Leggat? Who's Leggat?'

'Otto Leggat.'

And then the penny dropped. Otto Leggat, MP for one of the north-east constituencies, had been the defector of the decade. Son of a miner and an artist. Honours degree at Cambridge. Youngest-ever Minister of Defence and the pride and joy of the party. The Tory party. Loved by the Whips, the Cabinet, his fellow members, half the Opposition and all the Tory ladies. The eligible bachelor of all time.

Then the country woke up one morning to find that one of its Cabinet ministers had defected to Moscow. The headlines were thick, big, and black, and it was a Thursday, and at Prime Minister's Question Time the Opposition made hay. The PM himself, the Home Secretary and, despite protocol, half the Civil Service, were publicly put through the mincer. The

United States Government was horrified and nowhere in the Western world did anyone say 'I told you so.' Mainly because nobody had. The *Sunday Times* Insight team published no article on how the escape was contrived and after a few weeks of stunned reaction Leggat was publicly forgotten. As so often happened after some major tragedy or disaster, the Western world pulled down its mental shutters and got on with its normal strikes, murders and subversion. Even behind the scenes nothing much was known. Leggat had flown to Newcastle Airport by North-East Airlines, and after that there was no trace of him. To all intents and purposes he had never left the airport. But it was reported that at the Kremlin press conference Leggat looked tired and worn.

Felinski reached forward for Franks's empty cup as he said, 'How does this concern me?'

'Voronov knows why he went. And how.'

'Go on.'

'And Voronov can get him back.'

'And our lot want him back?'

'We know he can give us the whole of the KGB networks covering this country, "Legals" and "Illegals". Agents, cutouts, sleepers, codes, radio operators, dead-letter-boxes, "places of conspiracy", the lot.'

'So why doesn't Voronov bring him back?'

'It's a very dangerous operation, Steve; I'm sure you recognize that. Voronov won't do it for Maxwell or anyone else but you. Seems he trusts you. Believes only you and he can do it.'

Felinski's face was as impassive as ever but his hands were clenched aggressively.

'Let's get this straight. I'm a farmer. I'm a working farmer, not a dog and stick farmer, and I haven't the time to be involved in this sort of game, even if I had the inclination. Apart from anything else I'm no longer in my twenties; I'm old, Father William. Too old for these capers.'

Franks held up his hand to silence the flood. 'Steve, I know just how you feel. I'd feel the same myself.'

'But you are at least in the racket. It's your job.'

Franks said quietly, 'No, I'm not, Steve. I left five years ago. I grow my roses now in Surrey. They raked me out of bed last night. They're desperate and they're in a hurry.'

'I still don't see why the hurry.'

'Of course not. Would you give me a chance to tell you why it's so urgent?'

Felinski stood hands on hips looking at the man who was still composed, still talking quietly and calmly, and he couldn't wipe out his mental picture of the same man. The man who had worked for months to ensure that every detail of Felinski's operation in Germany was meticulously planned. The man who'd seen him trembling and shaking with fear before the flight. And the man whose name was on the recommendation that had made him Major Felinski, DSO. He sat down and nodded to Franks.

'OK. Tell me.'

'Was a thing called the "Special Collection" around in your day? I don't think it was.'

'No, I've never heard of it.'

'Well, it's a Soviet document. A collection of documents in fact. It is the views of the Soviet Ministry of Defence, chiefs of military academies, the General Staff, military planners and other experts on how to wage the next war. The Special Collection was started in 1960 and it is updated monthly. Right from the start it was accepted as a basic premise that if there *was* to be war against the USA, the Soviets must get in first. It's gone on from there. There was always only one country against which they were prepared to start a war – and that was the United States. Only defensive plans had been drawn up for all other contingencies – mainly China.

'In January 1973 the Soviets decided that it was essential to neutralize Europe before a pre-emptive strike against the USA could succeed. They also decided that neutralizing this country would neutralize Europe as a whole. After that they could attack the USA when they were ready.

'We have learned from Voronov that the subversion operation against this country will start very soon. So our people are much concerned, and of course the United States assume that this is the curtain-raiser to pre-emptive strikes against them. The Russian Embassy controls a network here, and there are signs that there may be two others. One controlled from Paris and the other from Dublin. We have no idea how long they expect to take to wreck this country, but if they succeed, then

57

according to the Special Collection the nuclear attack on the United States will follow automatically. Probably inside six months.

'Voronov is our key man in this, and as I've said, he'll now only work with you. Our people cannot avoid appealing for your help. There isn't even any incentive we can offer. You are already a wealthy man, you have work you enjoy, so all we can do is ask. There are no pressures, Steve. None at all.'

'And Leggat. What's his role?'

'Leggat helped them plan it.'

'Why does he want to come back then?'

'Wind up? Who knows? I guess it started as an interesting exercise and it now looks very real, very possible. I suspect it was hatred that made him go in the first place. And hatred dies away over the years. You end up only remembering the good bits.'

'You haven't said that I owe something to this country for providing refuge and shelter for my great-grandfather.'

'True. And we have no intention of saying so. Your family have repaid that debt many times over. You did yourself in Germany. That turned out well but it could easily have been otherwise. No pressure on that score.'

'What do we know about the KGB networks and their plans?'

'Oh we know a bit, we know a bit. If you took this on you'd have every possible assistance. I expect you realize that.'

'What about the farm?'

Franks leaned forward and touched Felinski's knee. 'Steve, I know that must mean you are at least considering it. Let me tell you what Maxwell had planned. Your cover for leaving the farm for some time was to be an exchange visit with an American farmer. They've tapped a genuine expert to come here and run the farm for you. Obviously we should see that you make at least as much as you make now, and he would be authorized to carry out any improvements involving capital that you agreed to.'

Felinski smiled, and Franks said, 'What is it, Steve?'

'I guess I must be the only man in the country who could be tempted to risk his neck for the sake of a concrete farm access road.'

Franks smiled too, but he knew he had said all that should be said.

Felinski stood up and walked slowly to the big farmhouse window. St Luke had come into his own. The sky was blue and there was a pale sun. On the big field seagulls were wheeling and diving, which meant there must be a high wind at the coast. He noticed a limping sheep and made a mental note to warn Bill Weeks of foot-rot. But young Mason *had* been right. He was bored. The problems of foot-rot and fowl-pest were real enough, but year in year out the same few problems cropped up and the same old answers sufficed. At dinner with the parson and his family the previous evening, he had realized that even they were more in the world than he was. Probably because of his wartime training and experience he *had* withdrawn, and he realized that he actually looked forward to the girl's visits, but couldn't bring himself to show it or admit it. He swung round to face Franks who had turned in his chair to look at him. He was conscious, as he spoke, of being impulsive, which went against his grain. But he was equally conscious that he wanted to be back in the racket. It felt like coming home.

'When do they want me to start?'

Franks gave a big sigh. 'Stephen, you don't know how relieved I am. Would you let Maxwell come and see you to-morrow? I hasten to add that you will run your own operation, but he's your liaison with the CIA. And he is very competent, I assure you.'

'Let's say Maxwell comes tomorrow about breakfast time – say eight o'clock?'

Chapter 9

There was a crowd at London airport to watch the departure of the Tupolev TU-144. There was first-class accommodation for eighteen passengers and eighty-two tourist class. It had come in on Friday evening, non-stop from Moscow, on its first regular flight, and reporters and TV crews had watched the twenty-five passengers descend from the high platform steps. Once again the Russians had done it. The TU-144, to the layman, looked like the Concorde. Air experts had noticed the different engine air-intake geometry and the repositioned undercarriage members.

It was taking forty passengers on the return journey and it would land in Moscow seventy-five minutes from take-off at Heathrow. Traffic Control had refused to modify the mandatory procedure for take-off, and the pilot was powering up the four Kuznetsov turbo-fans so that the ground staff and apron staff had to retreat to the shelter of the terminal buildings. As it roared down the main runway there were few who were not impressed.

Boris Yasnov closed the curtains across the aircraft window, opened his plastic case, and once more checked the contents. Underwear, shirts, razor and bits and pieces, camera, perfume, silk scarves, two packs of playing cards and a dozen dry batteries. The usual loot one brought back for friends in Moscow. The pale blue plastic file cover used for all top secret KGB papers was at the bottom of the case and his two passports were in his inside pocket.

There was already a thin layer of snow at Moscow and Yasnov trod carefully in his new Italian shoes. His car and driver were waiting for him and he was taken direct to his apartment in Granovsky Street. He'd been allotted the new apartment on his promotion to full colonel. The block housed generals and a couple of marshals, one of whom was Zhukov. There were other senior KGB officers, and a few from the Soviet military intelligence organization, the GRU. When he was given the new apartment he thought he would miss the freedom of his old place on Pushkin Street. He could do what he liked there, with no one to notice. With all the brass at Granovsky Street it could be a bit strait-laced. But it hadn't turned out like that. There was more drinking and womanizing than he would have believed. He fitted in well. One of his neighbours was Ivanov who worked for the GRU. He'd been the assistant Naval Attaché at the London Embassy until he'd got mixed up with the Profumo scandal. Ivanov had given him some telephone numbers that made his visits to London more interesting.

Boris Ivanovich Yasnov was born on 23 April 1919 in Kiev, the capital of the Ukraine. His father was an Armenian and his mother a Pole. His parents parted when he was seven and he was sent to a state home for orphans. He was a Komsomol member from 1937 until he became a cadet at the second Kiev Artillery School in 1939. He did so well that he was sent to the Frunze Military Academy in Khirgizia on the Chinese border. When, in July '41, he was personally selected to transfer to the NKVD by its head, Beria, it was certain that his career was going to be either very short or very successful. In two years he was deputy head of the Third Directorate, responsible for strategic intelligence covering the Anglo-American countries.

His experience operationally was wider than any other man in the KGB. He had controlled a network operating just over the Mexican border based on Mexicali, supplying information on defence establishments from San Diego to Santa Cruz. This was so successful that he had been pushed up to New York as Director of the main Soviet network in the United States. From a photo studio in Brooklyn he had controlled Rudolf Abel and Reino Hayhanen. It was his skilful use of Gerda Munsinger, operating as a call-girl in Montreal, that caused the uproar involving the Associate Defence Minister of Canada in 1966. There was still a special commendation in Yasnov's 'P' file at Central Registry. It praised his spare-time activity for the KGB – photographing tombstones in New York cemeteries so that the details could be used by the KGB in forged birth certificates and passports. Yasnov was not only a top-grade schemer, he was a grafter too and the KGB rated him highly.

When the drunken Hayhanen defected to the CIA station in Paris and exposed Abel as a KGB colonel, Yasnov had gone to ground. He had left New York for Washington. There he had organized and controlled a network into the Pentagon with a side penetration into the CIA. In 1969 he had been recalled to Moscow and had been controller of all operations in the United States and Britain. Most of the KGB's agents in America and Europe were not Soviet citizens. One of the drawbacks of the system was that the Russians' minds were so blinkered that they could never survive undetected in a free society. How could you undo years of Soviet propaganda about how they lived in the West? It was like a policeman waving a driver across a red light. When Lieutenant-Colonel Prikhodko had spoken at the seminar to introduce his Training Manual on the Characteristics of Agent Handling in the USA, he had given a rundown on American characteristics, and Yasnov was the only one of the assembled KGB top brass who'd burst out laughing at the statement that most Americans wore shoes two sizes too big. Afterwards, although they had been tactful to both parties, he had been forced to apologize to Prikhodko.

In July 1973, at the updating meeting for the Special Collection, they had the first sign of the Party taking a look at what the military were up to. There are only fifteen members of the Presidium since Stalin's death, and there are grey-haired generals and state functionaries who spend a lifetime without seeing a Presidium member. When, for the first time, one of them attended the Special Collection meeting, men who wielded great power had felt that their deliberations might be fruitless. The Presidium member had not spoken during the meeting. He had sat there impassively, listening but not taking notes. A point had been referred to him early in the discussion just to test the atmosphere. He hadn't even replied. He had shaken his head dismissively and had looked coldly at the questioner. The meeting had dragged to an end with the assembled top brass gradually getting the message. The Party didn't like where the Special Collection was heading for.

Almost due east of Moscow the main road from the city centre sweeps under the outer ring-road and turns slightly northward at Balashikha, and by Bezmenkovo the forests come down to border the road. There is a Red Air Force base ten miles farther on at Konino, but just before that a small road turns off due north. Five miles up that road is the small town of Kishkino, and on the northern edge of the town a dirt road leaves the main road and twists into the cool of the forest. A mile farther on there is a lake and on its northern shore there were lights reflected in the water from a long, low dacha. It was there that Marshals Rudovsky and Voroshilov waited for the Head of the Commissariat of State Security – the KGB. It was almost a month after the last Special Collection meeting.

It was nearly midnight when they finally saw the lights of his car as it swung round the edge of the lake. Vladimir Semichastny was alone, and as the three sat comfortably around a low teak table the two marshals waited for the KGB man to broach the subject of their meeting. Semichastny had a foot in both camps. He was not only the head of the KGB but was an alternative member of the Presidium. That had been part of Kruschev's peasant cunning to make sure that the KGB was really controlled by the Party. At least that had been his intention, and there had never been the need to test its reality. The Presidium made all decisions on policy, and sometimes on detail, of every aspect of the Soviets' military, economic, and foreign policy. But the KGB had the power to investigate, and act without hindrance from any source, in the same wide area. The Army, the GRU, the Party, and every committee, were ruthlessly policed by the KGB. And the Red Army and its colleagues in the Navy and Air Force represented the other great power block. And these three bases of power, the Party, the military, and the KGB, were like giant amoebae, constantly multiplying and dividing, joining and parting, as their several interests exerted their terrible pressures.

It was Voroshilov who finally tested the temperature.

'Well now, Vladimir, tell us what our masters have in mind.'

Semichastny put down his glass on the table and reached for a cigarette. He took his time lighting it and as he leaned back in his chair he half closed his eyes as he exhaled.

'They don't like the Special Collection.'

It was Rudovsky who spoke, 'But it's been basically the same for a year. More – maybe eighteen months. Why all this now?'

Semichastny looked across at Rudovsky. 'Comrade Marshal, they've changed their minds. When a pre-emptive strike against the Americans was a plan, they didn't mind. When it becomes an ongoing operation they *do* mind. When I had my talk with Litkov it was clear that they are scared. His exact words were, "They've gone too far. They've made a plan into an operation", and that's what it's all about.'

Rudovsky couldn't conceal his anger. 'So why didn't they say so? Why send that idiot Litkov to the meeting? Sitting there like a bloody sphinx, saying nothing but looking as if we were criminals or naughty boys.'

Semichastny smiled and shrugged. 'You should know them by now, comrade. They don't want to be stuck with the blame if they abandon the Special Collection and then find later that their alternative policy goes sour and the Americans kick us in the teeth when we could have done it to them first.'

'And what the hell is their alternative?'

Semichastny glanced at Voroshilov and saw the half-smile and kept his temper. 'Comrade Rudovsky, we have been talking *détente* with the Americans for months, you know that. It was meant to give us time. Now they think it's actually working. More than half the Presidium believe that *détente* is now possible.'

'They must be bloody mad.'

Semichastny laughed. 'They like the power, Marshal, like the rest of us. They don't want to risk losing it. Even the others who are doubtful are convinced that a pre-emptive strike is possibly unnecessary.'

'So we kill the Special Collection. A plan worked out by the best strategists in the Soviet Union. Not just as the best plan but the only plan.'

'No. That's where you're wrong. They don't propose killing it. They'll let you all carry on planning and talking. You can make the locomotive but you mustn't put it on the railway lines. That's all.'

Rudovsky was red-faced with anger. 'What do they think we are? We play games just to keep them happy. Not me. That's out – absolutely out.'

'So what will you do, comrade?'

'I'll resign and tell them they're fools, or traitors, or both.'

Semichastny sighed and reached for his glass. 'If you do that, comrade, you'd end up my guest in the Lubyanka.'

Voroshilov had said nothing as the two had talked. He'd once been a member of the Presidium and one word that Semichastny had used had told him all he needed to know. You didn't talk about members of the Presidium being scared if you were scared too. You didn't need to be a politician or a diplomat to find a more tactful word than 'scared'. He stretched and yawned, and walked slowly over to the big window. He stood there with one hand in his pocket and the other parting the heavy velvet curtains. The moon was summer white and almost full, and a path of light lay on the lake and ended where the old wooden jetty jutted out from the rushes that edged the banks. A long flat punt was tied to the jetty and he could see the pair of small oars and the hump of the box that held the live-bait. Without turning, he spoke quietly but clearly.

'What do we do, Vladimir?'

There was silence for a moment, and he turned slowly, his eyes on Semichastny's face. The younger man didn't avoid his gaze but it was almost a minute before he spoke.

'We go on, comrade. We go on.'

Voroshilov pulled back a chair and loosened his tunic before he sat down.

'And the KGB will be with us?'

Semichastny nodded. 'All the way.'

'And the Special Collection meetings?'

'We carry on holding them but there are no longer any time factors introduced. We keep it as a plan. We don't put it on the railway lines. We stay good boys. Eager but obedient. Nothing gets said. We just take the hint.'

Voroshilov smiled. 'And?'

'And we start the subversion operation.'

Rudovsky looked startled. 'The subversion operation? What's that?'

Voroshilov chipped in quickly. 'That's the preliminary. Before we tackle the Americans we want Europe neutralized.' He laughed. 'Or preferably paralysed. Our friend here is looking after that. When we've done that we'll look at the Special Collection again.' He turned to Semichastny. 'Who's going to be in charge of that, comrade?'

'Yasnov.'

'He was the one in America?'

'That's the man. We've done a new appreciation and we're going to concentrate on the British.'

Rudovsky shifted in his seat and nodded as if in agreement. 'What's it all about, Voroshilov?'

Voroshilov waved a hand at Semichastny who poured himself another drink.

'We want to separate Europe from the Americans. We've got plans for France and Italy, but Britain is what matters.'

'Why them?'

'No matter what anyone says, they've got a special relationship with the Americans. That doesn't mean they always like each other. They've got a special relationship with the Irish and they hate one another's guts. It's hard to define. Could be the common language, could be because that's where the Pilgrim Fathers came from. Whatever the reason, it exists.

'If Italy went Communist tomorrow the Americans wouldn't be shocked too much. If France went Communist they'd be shocked, but they wouldn't do anything active about it, beyond doubling the CIA's budget. But if Britain went Communist the Americans would batten down the hatches and let Europe go hang.

'The same thing applies with the other European countries. If Britain went Communist, whether it was by elections or revolution, the rest of Europe would follow. They're ready for it now. The country's split down the middle. The trades unions against the rest. Our people have been doing a good job there for the last ten years. A little push and they'll be over the edge. But it's vital that it's co-ordinated and planned.

'On top of all this, you've got to bear in mind that with Ireland out and Britain out the Americans are finished in the North Atlantic. They'd have a wide-open flank on their most strategically important front.

'There's no doubt, comrade, that Britain's the key to throwing Europe *and* the United States off balance. And what's more, they know it. They'll do anything to stop real trouble in Britain.'

Voroshilov stood up. 'Come on, you two. Let's get to bed if we're fishing tomorrow.'

. . . . .

Boris Yasnov was a handsome man. A rather heavy face with big gentle, brown eyes. About five feet ten inches, his broad shoulders and big hands made him look stockier than he really was. His short hair was black, so black that it shone. He was smartly dressed even by New York standards, and, like downtrodden workers who prefer working for a boss with a Bentley, the snappy dresser was rather admired by his peers in the KGB. He was their boy who took on the Americans, the one who knew how to operate in their capitalistic jungle. He was personally disliked by many as an all-round bastard, but none envied him his assignments in the West.

Chapter 10

He'd watched Maxwell park his car in the space by the silo and walk back along the road to the farmhouse gate, then up the flagged path. There were to be no more surprise visits.

Felinski took Maxwell into his study and they sat facing one another at the oak table. Maxwell started. 'I apologize for the other night; I guess I'd got my motivations mixed up.' Seeing Felinski's raised eyebrows, he went on, 'They'd told me you were an informal sort of guy. I'd got to wait for you, so I decided you wouldn't mind if I invited myself in. And then I guess the old CIA instincts took over and I thought I'd check out how you reacted after all these years.' He grinned. 'I sure found that out.'

'Shall we talk about Voronov?'

'OK. Voronov contacted the CIA office in Berlin, West Berlin that is. That was nearly four months ago. He was testing the temperature for a walk-out and we finally did a deal and he came over a couple of weeks later. He gave us enough to clear up a couple of networks in Berlin and one in Bonn. I think he was holding back about Leggat until he'd satisfied himself about us.

'I've been running him and I thought we'd been doing fine. Then he told me about Leggat wanting out and he laid it on the line that he could do it, but only with you. I pressured him a bit but he wasn't buying it. That's where we are now.'

'How did he come into contact with Leggat?'

'Wouldn't say a word. Matter of fact he wouldn't say where he worked with you.'

'It was in Germany.'

'Is that a fact? By the way, my name's Bill and I know yours is Steve.'

'Did he say anything else about Leggat?'

'Just what I told your people. Says Leggat has all the details of the two main KGB networks in this country. Leggat will trade those if we lift him out and have him back.'

'Have him back openly or under cover?'

'No idea what he wants.'

68

'Where's Voronov now?'

'Well, this is where we tread a bit carefully. Back at CIA Langley they naturally consider Voronov as ours. That was fine till this Leggat business cropped up. When this jazz about only working with you started, my brass got a bit touchy. They weren't sure how SIS would react, so I shipped Voronov back to the States, just as a small precaution. But it's all been cleared for you to talk with him there, and I'm pretty sure they'll release him to you if you're satisfied with his story. Your people think he's still in Berlin.'

'What part do you want in this, Maxwell – Bill?'

'Well, CIA are deeply concerned, as you can guess. Although this part happens here, it looks like it's only a prelude to wiping us out – or trying to.'

'And?'

'They'll want me to be informed. I'll want to know everything your people know.'

'Just that?'

'Yes. We'll give you a hundred per cent co-operation. Any way you want it. But it's already been agreed that it's your operation.'

'Not a joint operation?'

'Not unless you request it or it starts going bad.'

'When can I see Voronov?'

Maxwell looked at his watch. 'I can get a chopper here in twenty minutes. Say thirty minutes to Northolt and you can be in New York – say four hours from now. We'd use an F one eleven E.'

'I've got things to do, Bill. How about you lay on transport for me tomorrow morning at eleven, at Lydd?'

'Lydd? That's the cross-Channel airfield near here, isn't it?'

'That's it.'

'OK. I'll come down for you at eleven.'

When Maxwell had gone, Felinski reached for the phone and dialled the Mermaid Hotel in Rye and asked for Franks.

'Hello, Steve. How did it go?'

'Reasonable. I need to get that exchange farmer quickly.'

'Fine. I gather he's already at the US Embassy cooling his heels. He can be with you in a couple of hours. I'll pick him up at Hastings station. Anything else?'

'Yes, I want funds.'
'You can pick those up in town tomorrow.'
'No, I'm leaving from Lydd mid-morning.'
'I see. How long'll you be away?'
'No idea. I'll have to play it by ear.'
'Pounds do?'
'No, dollars.'
'Leave it to me. Say two thousand?'
'That'll do.'

Felinski showed the American his farm records and introduced him to Bill Weeks. The take-over took an hour and the American was calling in the next morning at eight. Franks brought the money with him. He also gave Felinski a London contact telephone number, and a recognition signal.

When they had gone he phoned through to the rectory at Tenterden. Lavender Coombs herself answered and was delighted to be invited to dinner that night.

They had eaten well and he drove her back to the farm. The curtains were drawn and the fire had warmed the room. As he poured them a drink she said, 'Hey fatso, you've drawn the curtains. You never draw the curtains, Steve. Are you going to seduce me?'

'Here's a drink. Sit down, I want to talk to you.'

She smiled. 'You know you don't need to say a word. I'm ready when you are.'

He sighed and sipped at his whisky. She held up her glass and said 'Na zdrowie'. And he smiled because she'd remembered the Polish salutation he'd taught her.

'Lavender.'

'Yes.'

'Can we be serious for a minute?'

She looked up quickly and he could see the anxiety in her eyes. 'When people say that it means it's going to be nasty.'

'Will you marry me?'

She put down her glass and he saw her hand shaking. But she looked across at him intently and said very softly, 'We're not playing games any more are we, Steve?'

He shook his head.

'The answer's yes. But I want to ask two questions. But whatever your answers are, the answer is still yes.'

'Why ask questions, then?'

'I'm a girl, Steve. I need to know.'

'Ask on then.'

'Why do you want me to marry you?'

'I've cared about you ever since you were a little girl and for a long time I've loved you without knowing. Or maybe without acknowledging it. I love your honesty and generosity and I'd like you to be around here all the time. Apart from that there are things I'd like to do to you that are probably best done when we're married. Any more questions?'

'Why do you ask me tonight?'

'Because I have to go away tomorrow morning. It's an exchange visit with an American farmer, arranged way back but it's come up suddenly. I don't know how long I'll be away, maybe as long as two months. It's a bit selfish but I wanted a prize to go with.'

She half smiled. 'That's the first time since I've been grown-up that you haven't been truthful with me. Because I know you, I know there'll be a good reason. And it won't be selfish either.'

Lavender Coombs was wearing a white silk dress with a pattern of big red roses and there was no doubt she was a woman not a girl, despite the pleasure in the bright blue eyes, and the beaming smile. He went over and sat beside her and took her hand.

'I expect you'll hear all the warnings about Spring marrying Autumn and all that stuff. Will it worry you?'

She shook her head. 'Not the slightest. I don't think I'll get much of that. I think everyone expected it. Except you, of course.' He kissed her gently and when they pulled apart she said softly, 'Do you want to make love to me?'

He took her hand in both of his. 'Yes, I want to. But we won't. We'll wait till I come back. I'll want to take a long, long time. Days if not weeks.'

And not long afterwards he'd driven her back to the rectory.

'I'll walk back, Lavender. I'll leave the MG for you to use. I'll enjoy thinking about you using her. It'll be a kind of link for me.'

Chapter 11

The F-111E had come in well to the west of Kennedy International Airport and was doing an elliptical circuit from Raritan Bay to Jersey City. When they were given clearance they came over Bayonne Military Terminal, across Upper Bay, and they were over Owls Head Park as the undergear thumped down. They landed at Floyd Bennett Field and parked alongside a small flock of Navy helicopters.

There was a car waiting for them, and after some minor formalities they were being driven fast up Flatbush Avenue. They finally headed over Manhattan Bridge and turned on to the Franklin D. Roosevelt Driveway. Almost twenty minutes later they edged into Sutton Place. The apartment was on the eighteenth floor and the big picture windows gave a magnificent view across the East River.

Maxwell ordered a meal for both of them and Felinski noticed that Maxwell, on his home ground, was the man of authority and action. They were finishing the wine when Maxwell said, 'I'd like to suggest that we turn in fairly early so you get a chance to get over the time lag.'

'Suits me.'

Maxwell was fiddling with his wine glass and he didn't look up when he said, 'If you want a girl, Steve, you just say the word.'

'Thanks, Bill. How about meeting Voronov?'

'I had in mind tomorrow morning just before lunch.'

'Fine. How is he these days?'

Maxwell leaned back, stretching. 'I don't know what he was like way back but now he's a pretty tough specimen. When he was operating in East Berlin for the KGB he gave us some very hard knocks. I suspect that two of our agents who were killed were killed by Voronov. I don't mean on his orders, I mean killed by him personally.'

'As a matter of interest, did you offer him a woman?'

'Sure we did. He's been working through them in alphabetical order.'

'When he came over to you, what did he give as his reasons?'

'He said he wanted a better deal than he got with the Soviets. I think that's pretty well true. We put him through the mangle for a couple of weeks. You can see the transcripts if you want. We had him on the lie-detector most of the time. He had spent very little time in the Soviet Union after he went back and he'd lost his feelings for the country. They broke a few promises and I think that mattered. His parents died some years back and they hadn't got a grip on him any more. I understand he was promised an Order and nothing happened. They don't pay nationals too well either, as you know.'

When Voronov came into the big room the sun was shining and the light exaggerated the deep lines on his face. He stood in the doorway for a moment and then as he saw Felinski he came forward, his big hand outstretched.

'Stephen.'

'Kliment.'

And the big bear of a man wrapped his arms round Felinski and kissed him on both cheeks. There was no doubt that he was delighted to see Felinski again. With a few minutes of small talk Felinski got down to business. They talked in Russian for Voronov's benefit and when Felinski had changed over Voronov had said, smiling, 'You talking Russian because you think they've bugged this place?'

'I'm sure it's bugged. And I'm sure they have Russian-speaking employees. Anyway you work for them now and my people are co-operating with them on this case.'

Voronov nodded and grinned.

'So tell me about Leggat.'

Voronov shook his head. 'First you tell me about you.'

'I'm in charge of this operation. Is that what you mean?'

'Nobody can give you orders?'

'Almost nobody.'

'Nobody in Security I mean.'

'No. I've got a free hand.'

'OK. Then we talk. Well, I did some work with Leggat when he worked for the State Committee for the Co-ordination of Scientific Research Work. I set up a network for him dealing with industrial espionage. It operated into West Germany. We

73

spent a lot of time together over a period of about ten months. I told him about my co-operation with the English in Hanover. And he told me a bit about his life in Government and so on . . .'

Felinski interrupted, 'What was his attitude to the British?'

Voronov looked across at Felinski and didn't answer immediately. 'It wasn't normal.'

'In what way?'

'Political defectors, ideological defectors, are always full of praise for the Soviet system and they can't say enough bad about their own régimes. They genuinely feel this way in the early stages and later on they've *got* to think it or they acknowledge that they were hoodwinked.'

'And Leggat?'

'Leggat was like a married man who commits adultery with a beautiful girl he lusts after, and then discovers that he prefers his wife. There were constant comparisons between your way of life and the Soviet way of life and I had the feeling that he preferred your way, but that he'd only just discovered this feeling. Maybe I'm wrong about the adultery man. Let's say he was like a man who gets a divorce and then keeps telling his new wife how the first wife looked after the home so well. It was not so definite as I describe it but I'm sure that's how it was.'

'Was it just nostalgia, Kliment? The green fields of old England stuff?'

Voronov shook his head and stubbed out his cigarette. 'No. Definitely not. Burgess and Maclean and to some extent Philby were like that. Always talking about their clubs, and parties, cricket and so on. But they wanted the Soviet system in England, still keeping all the other things. Leggat was a bloodstream Communist who wasn't impressed with the Soviet system when he saw it.'

'Well lots of fellow travellers and lefties aren't impressed when they see it in practice.'

'Yes, but this man had had power in England. Real power. He wasn't an emotional cripple who wanted to go to Mother Russia. He's got a brain like a knife and his analysis of capitalism and the Soviets was precise.'

Voronov paused, and Felinski sensed that he was being given time to grasp something important. But he couldn't sort out the material.

74

'Have you got any clues about what makes Leggat tick?'

He saw Voronov reach for his inside pocket. He pulled out a card and pencil and as Felinski watched, Voronov wrote something on the card while he was talking.

'No, he's an odd sort of man, but I've no doubt that he wants to come back if your people will let him.'

Voronov pushed the card across the shining table-top to Felinski and he read what Voronov had written.

It said, 'Leggat isn't English. Keep talking.'

Felinski put the card in his pocket.

'Why does he want to come back?'

'He was very cagey. Said he'd had enough and regretted what he had done. There's more to it than that, of course. I think he'd tell you but not me. Probably misses the fleshpots.'

'And what about the deal?'

'A complete exposure of the subversion operation in Britain.'

'You think he can deliver?'

'I'm sure he can. He organized and planned most of it with the KGB.'

'Let's go and find some fresh air.'

When they were down in Sutton Place, Felinski laughed. 'You know, I don't even remember what day it is.'

'It's Sunday.'

'Let's get a taxi to Central Park.'

The sun was warm and they walked from the corner of 5th and 59th and took a bench by the skating rink.

'Tell me about Leggat; what's it all about? There's something wrong somewhere in that story.'

'Nothing wrong in the story, comrade. What's wrong comes at the beginning. Leggat is not his real name and he's not English either.'

'For God's sake, what is he then?'

'Old man Leggat lived in one of the London suburbs. He was a printer. Had his own small business. Joined the Party in the very early days. He was given a holiday in Moscow just before the war, about 1938 I think it was. They gave him a job to do. Soon after he got back he sold his business and left the district. He moved to the other side of the river and set up another printing outfit. In Croydon somewhere. About that time he was joined by a youngster, supposedly his brother's boy, he was about seventeen then, maybe sixteen. The brother had settled in Australia after the first war. The boy went to university, to Oxford, and did well.

'The rest you probably know because that was Otto Leggat. Except that his real name is Pyatokov. The brother did have a son, two in fact. But one died very young and it was his birth certificate they used. The Moscow Centre had arranged the deal with Leggat while he was in Moscow and young Pyatokov was "planted" for future use. Old man Leggat was the only one who knew he was a plant. Outside Moscow that is. He was put here as a "sleeper", and they had no idea he would become a Minister in a government. They didn't use him for a long time, probably only the last four years he was in England.'

'Why did he do a bolt?'

'Well, old man Leggat died about 1960 or 1961. A heart attack. That meant that Otto was on his own. Almost a perfect cover now. Except for the old man's brother in Australia and his other son. If you check the records you'll find that that son died in Singapore in 1942 in Changi Camp. That left only his father, Leggat's brother. He's still alive as far as I know. Lives in Kiev. They did a deal with him after old man Leggat died. Paid his passage, gave him a good job, and then retired him. He lives well. He wasn't even a Communist.'

'So why did Leggat – Pyatokov – go back?'

'One of the TV companies was going to do a big piece on friend Otto. Most of the newspapers had done potted histories, but this was going to be a big production. A team went to Australia to cover the background and they got busy trying to trace the father. They started checking in Emigration and a clerk there tipped off our Embassy. They decided in Moscow that Otto was going to be exposed. He was ordered to get out at once.'

'How did he leave?'

'Holy Mother, I can't remember. I think he went from somewhere in the north-east by boat to Denmark, and then by plane to Moscow.'

'Have you got contact with Leggat now?'

'Not direct. Through CIA I have. But I think they do it through your people – SIS.'

'Is he under special surveillance?'

'I don't know about now, but he wasn't when I was there. Just routine. After all he's a national, and a Hero of the Soviet Union.'

'Is this operation based on the existing KGB network in England?'

'The normal network in the UK is controlled from Paris but there's a second network in Dublin and that's controlled from the new Russian Embassy in the Republic. That gives them easy entrance to your country. No passports, no movement control. I'd guess they will be using both. There could be a special team involved as well.'

'Does that mean they're using Irish nationals?'

'I've no idea. I should think so. But Leggat can tell us.'

'If we needed to contact Leggat without going through CIA and SIS, could you do that?'

Voronov studied Felinski's face for a moment and then grinned. 'I would need two days. But yes, I could do that.'

'Let's go back.'

When they got back to the apartment Maxwell was there with two other men, and as Voronov and Felinski came in, the group, who were talking near the window, fell silent. Then Maxwell came forward.

'Steve, Kliment, let me introduce you. This is General Healey and this is Peter Bonetti.'

The General looked like a general, an American general anyway. He looked far too young to be a general in Europe. He was tanned, which made the green eyes look even darker, and there were creases around his mouth that could have been from smiling but could have been from something quite different. His hand was dry and sandpapery and his grip was not overdone.

Bonetti was tall and slim, and despite his name his hair was blond. He bowed but didn't offer his hand. He wore a dark blue suit, broad-striped fashionable shirt and a modish big tie. His smile was amiable but professional. Could be upper-echelon IBM or a genuine Boston Brahmin. Or both.

Maxwell waved them to the big table and poured drinks and handed them round. When they were all settled he said, 'I thought we should have a little meeting, Steve. General Healey is from Strategic Planning and Peter Bonetti is CIA. We'd like to give you a bit of background.' He grinned as he raised his glass. 'Background from our point of view this time. You go first, General.'

Healey nodded and placed his hands gently, palms down, on the green baize cover. He looked for a moment at his hands, and then looked up at Felinski.

'I want to explain the current position on missiles. These days that's all that matters. Troops and the rest of it are virtually show-biz now. It's missiles and anti-missiles that will put the nails in the coffins. You may know some of what I'm going to tell you; if so, forgive me.

'If the Soviets fire an ICBM, an inter-continental ballistic missile, at us, it will take roughly thirty minutes from launch to impact. It'll be the same, more or less, if we fire at them. So, if we then come to anti-missile missiles, both sides have to knock down an enemy ICBM on the fifteen-minute line or earlier. We can both more or less do that, we're slightly up on them but nothing spectacular. And that looks like we cancel out. But that's not the fact. That thirty minutes is equal for a first-strike OK, but not as a defence. With rockets fuelled and ready to go, we're equal. But that's not the case for defensive action like anti-missile missiles. The Soviets have a crude and clumsy fuel to cope with compared with ours. We can knock down one of their ICBMs four minutes from launch – but they couldn't stop our current ICBMs from landing. If they made a permanent stand-to situation with just six of their anti-missile missiles it would cost them a million dollars a day of stand-to time. And if they then stood them down it would cost another million per missile.' He looked at Felinski's face carefully. 'You understand that?' Felinski nodded and Healey went on.

'We've had this status for forty-five weeks. To be more precise we have *potentially* had this status for that time. When my command evaluated the situation we recommended that we halt the manufacture and development of our new series missiles. Now let me tell you why.

'Ignoring the Soviets' stand-to costs we're almost equally balanced at the moment. We've got a slight edge but it's very marginal. Probably disappear in combat conditions after the first wave of ICBMs. The other boys knew this and we let it be known that we were putting the development and production of the new weapons in moth-balls.

'They've had two real top military and scientific missions over here in the last eight weeks and we've let them see anything in that area they wanted to see. We've done all we can to show 'em we're holding still. The Pentagon don't go all the way with this thinking but the White House laid it on the line. So that's what I have to tell you gentlemen.'

Maxwell came in quickly. 'I'd like Peter to talk first and then if you've got any questions we'll go over them. Peter.'

Bonetti had big brown eyes and as he looked at him Felinski wondered what women would make of those liquid, spaniel eyes. But they were alert eyes and they took in Voronov as well as Felinski, which is more than the General's had done.

'So we arrive at a near balance. An acceptable balance, and both sides have been careful to maintain that balance even in areas away from missiles. With China *we* have been cautious, in South Vietnam *they* have been cautious. In the Middle East both powers have tried to damp down the situation where it is within their power to do so. The strategic arms talks in Vienna have been inconclusive but that has satisfied both sides. The diplomacy on both sides has been the diplomacy of *détente*. Up to now, that is. What Voronov has told us is causing serious disquiet in the White House. The general tenor of the Special Collection we have been aware of. But we've done similar studies. The general subversion that goes on in Britain we take as normal. You people can cope with that. But a hard subversion operation with direct connections to the Special Collection, that's a new ball-game as far as we are concerned. That's how it all would start if they had in mind a pre-emptive strike against the US.

'We take it seriously enough for a number of special nuclear units to be stood-to. We've done it as quietly as possible but they'll spot it inside a month.

'So we want you, Mr Felinski, to understand that in leaving you in control of this situation it is not a question of being gracious, it's because we look to you to rip this thing apart. And quickly. We don't understand why they've changed tactics. Maybe they haven't. Or maybe there are two factions struggling for power. Whatever it is, we're desperate to know.

It's vital to United States security. So it's not just knocking this operation out, we need to know what's cooking. Is that understood?'

There was a silence and Felinski heard an aircraft in the distance. Then he said, 'What co-operation can I expect from the CIA?'

Maxwell chipped in fast. 'Anything. Anything you want. The same applies to the NSA and the FBI.'

'Anything that you people already know, that I've not been told for security reasons?'

Bonetti half-smiled and shook his head. 'No. What about you?'

Felinski's instincts were working overtime. 'There's one item that is going to create some friction between our two governments. But my people don't even know it yet. Nevertheless I'll tell you if holding it back will do any damage between us.'

Bonetti leaned back in his chair and looked at Maxwell, who looked over at Felinski. 'You mean Leggat's identity?'

Felinski knew then that either he, or Voronov, or both of them, must have been followed and subjected to some radio device, but he didn't wait to work it out. 'That's what I meant. It's going to embarrass our security people, it's going to make your people suspicious again. On the other hand if we get him out he's going to be right up to date on what's going on in the KGB regarding Britain.'

They weren't convinced, but nobody said so, and they discussed for an hour what the CIA had on file concerning the KGB in Great Britain.

Chapter 12

The safe-house in Curzon Street had a door that most people would never notice despite the fact that it was painted a brilliant gloss white and had bright brass furniture. It wasn't noticeable because it was between two shops, and had no number, and appeared to lead nowhere. It led, in fact, to a long narrow passage and another door. A man in a white roll-top sweater and denims opened the outer door when Felinski rang, and he led him back to the second door. It gave on to a small office with typewriter and desk and filing cabinets. The man in the white sweater stopped and with a smile said, 'I'm Tim. Tim MacNay. Can I see your passport?'

Felinski handed it over and it was checked carefully. Then MacNay handed it back. 'They're waiting for you.' And he opened a door whose green hessian covering matched perfectly the same covering on the walls. He saw Franks and two other men at a polished round table. A big-built man with a red face and grey wavy hair stood up and held out his hand. 'So glad you could come. I'm Clayton – SIS. This is Lomax from Special Branch and I asked my old friend Franks along because I thought you might like that. Now let's all sit down. By the way, Tim here is also SIS, and he'll be your routine contact. But mind you, we're all available, there's no protocol, no red-tape stuff.'

He waved Felinski to one of the chairs set round the table, and as Clayton leaned forward Felinski realized who he reminded him of. He was the spitting image of the previous Archbishop of Canterbury. The same rather old-womanish face, deceptively genial, and the alert blue eyes. The same hesitant searching for the really appropriate word.

'Can you tell us what you plan to do, Steve? Is it Steve or Stephen?'

'Steve is fine, sir. Voronov was not sure if the contact to Leggat was through SIS direct or via CIA.'

'It's not really direct but there's no need to go through CIA.

We can make contact through the Moscow Embassy but it takes about two days.'

'Voronov has a code arranged with Leggat and we're in the position that Leggat won't budge an inch except with Voronov, and *he* will only do it if I hold his hand.' Clayton and Lomax both nodded agreement. 'But before we start the engines there's something I want to tell you.'

And he gave them the full story of Leggat and his background. Nobody spoke when he had finished and they all looked at Felinski as if he had more to say. So he went on. 'This is obviously a policy matter outside my province but my attitude has been that, no matter who he is or what he is, he has information which we need quickly and that is all that matters.'

Clayton leaned back in his chair looking into space and then after a few moments he said, without turning his head, 'I agree. It's a dreadful shambles but we must ignore it. You just go ahead, but ...' and he struggled to sit upright again. As he turned to look at Felinski, there was a grimness of mouth that was not in any way benevolent. Clayton went on, '... but I must say this. When we've got what we want, then comrade Leggat is to be dealt with. Play along all you like till then but afterwards we deal with him.' And he nodded his head in emphasis.

'In that case, sir, I want a message to the Embassy contact immediately. I'll code it in Voronov's code and I'd like it to go to the second drop. The one in Gorky Park.'

'Fair enough, but we'll fix for *you* to contact the Embassy and then there'll be nothing outside your control. Now there's a small flat here, on the next floor, and I suggest you make that your base now. Tim here will be your admin man, he can lay on anything you need. Money, facilities, specialists, bodies – anything. Keep me informed.'

The TV camera showed the rather long face, and because of the lighting and the colour, it had the appearance of a medieval portrait by one of the van Eycks, of a bishop or a master-weaver. The mouth was square, but it was hard to decide whether the squareness came from determination or dentures. But it was the eyes that made the face mysterious. They seemed to be focused not on the camera, but on some private infinity. The look of a man who lived with desert horizons.

The interviewer said, 'And what will the union do now, Mr O'Connor?'

'That will depend on the Executive. I'm only an individual, I carry out the membership's will.' The voice was high-pitched but not strident.

'And when will the Executive meet?'

'On Tuesday.'

'Isn't that wasting a lot of time, with the strike date so near?'

'The Prime Minister took two days to decide to see us. It's our turn now.' And for the first time the eyes showed emotion. It was hard anger.

'And what about the public, Mr O'Connor?'

'They must blame the Prime Minister – the Government. It's them who're stiff-necked. They have the power to settle. All they've got to do is pay us a living wage.'

'The Government have offered you a twenty per cent increase already which you have refused.'

'I haven't refused, my members have refused. With deductions it would reduce it to seven quid extra take-home pay not ten.'

'But we all pay taxes, Mr O'Connor. Are you suggesting that your members' pay should be free of tax?'

The face was red with anger. 'You little bastard, don't you try taking the piss out of me. This interview's off. Forget it.' And he sat there like a child in a tantrum. The lights went out, but a sharp voice said, 'Put those lights back on at once.' They came on, and a tall, thin man who had been leaning against the door came over to join the two men in front of the camera. He looked down at the interviewer. 'We'll cut that last question. Cover why O'Connor thinks the Government are responsible and bring it to an end.'

'OK Chief.'

O'Connor leaned back in his chair and the tall, thin director pulled back the camera to include a framed photograph on the mantelpiece of O'Connor and his wife as bride and groom, and, above it, a pottery duck impaled on the wall.

'Why do you feel the Government is responsible for the present impasse, Mr O'Connor?'

'They came in on the working man's vote and it's time they looked after us.'

'Well, we all hope that some solution will be found to this and other union problems, and we shall be seeking *your* views later this evening in our special edition of "Today's World". when a representative panel will discuss the current state of industrial relations in Britain. Until then, this is Frank Maze – "Today's World".'

The TV team took almost half an hour to clear their equipment from the small semi-detached house in Croydon and when they were finished the director said, 'Sally, I want you to stay behind with me. Frank, when you get back, leave it all on tape and I'll edit it myself. See you in an hour. I've got my car here.'

When they had gone he sat down in one of the small armchairs. 'Mike, that was bloody stupid.'

'He was just trying to goad me.'

'Maybe he was, but you don't need to fall for it. Sally, tell me about that union leader directive. I heard about it as I was leaving.'

'It's pretty sweeping, John. In future when there is a major industrial relations problem likely to end in a strike, there will be no interviews of union leaders or industrial leaders. Only the general secretaries of the TUC and CBI can be interviewed. And only in general terms, not on the current problem.'

'Any reasons given?'

'Yes. The broadcast media are considered to be stirring things up by biased interviewing. And they are also accused of provoking wild statements which get turned into policy to save faces.'

John Fergus, one of Capitol TV's most experienced current affairs directors, stretched his long legs and looked across at O'Connor. 'You'll be on the panel tonight and I want you to raise the question of this directive. Indicate that you've heard about it from someone in the House. You know how to react. Muzzling the media, free speech, defend to the death any man's right et cetera, et cetera.'

O'Connor pursed his lips. 'Have you cleared all this with the Party?'

Fergus's face went stony. 'Don't try and come the old acid

with me, O'Connor. Just do what I've told you.' He stood up and stretched.

'Come on Sally. We'd better be making tracks.'

That evening at 10.19 viewers saw the first occasion when a TV show degenerated into violence on the screen. For some reason the cameras stayed on the scene of screaming women and fighting men. They saw it for seven minutes before the programme was cut and a nature film was substituted. It made the front page of every national newspaper the next morning. Two papers noted drily that the substitute film was a study of the family life of baboons. At least two editors wondered how the still photographs sent them by a Fleet Street agency had been taken on the spur of the moment. Who had tipped off whom? And why?

Chapter 13

The tall man wore only a short silk dressing-gown. The younger man, lying on the bed, was naked.

When he had finished pouring a drink from the decanter the tall man walked over to the bed and sat down. His hair was black but there were grey wings at the sides and under his chin were the tell-tale outriders of a dewlap. He looked at the young man and was terribly aware of the broad shoulders and the carved chest that gave on to the tensed pectoral muscles and the marble flat, young belly. Instinctively he reached forward and laid his hand lightly on the bulge of the young man's sex.

'When can you visit me again, Tony?'

The young man shrugged. 'I think they not let me have time till Saturday, Mr Vane.'

The older man sipped his drink slowly and there were tears in his eyes. He put down the glass carefully, and turning to the young man he said, 'Why don't you come and live here, Tony? We could spend more time together and you could have a better life.'

'I'm still counted as an alien, Mr Vane. They give me permit for this job and if I move they have to give permission. If I come here they say I not working and I must go.'

'You can be my personal assistant. I can fix all that.' And as his fingers gently stroked the blond pubic hair he said, 'I'll pay you, Tony, more than you get now.' And as the tears came again he said, 'I love you, Tony. I can't live without you.'

The young man struggled up on to his elbows. 'Don't be upset, Mr Vane. We'll see what we can do. You want to do it again before I leave, Mr Vane?'

Sir Andrew Pawson Vane, Eton and Oriel, had won his DSO at Anzio. His family owned several thousand acres just north of Berwick on Tweed. He was one of those charmers who seemed always to have the right qualifications at the right place at the right time. His marriage had not been successful but it had not ended in rancour on the front pages of the tabloids. He still saw Jessica and the girls, and their liking for him was not a patina of civilization, it was real. Only his family had seen his body after the flamethrower had gouged out the terrifying gap from his hip to his arm-pit. The metal-ribbed corset hid, and eased, the pain of the purple, melted flesh. Despite the terrible wound, his father remembered him saying that he had liked his time in the Army. He had seemed so at home with soldiers.

There had been no financial need for a career but there was a tradition of duty. His father's was to tenants and his became a duty to constituents in a Midlands industrial town.

He had charm and genuine affection for a wide circle of friends but he had love only for the young man who had just left. Laslo Gabor had come to England as a young boy with his parents. It had been 1956 and the second Hungarian uprising. Both his parents were middle-level operatives for the KGB, and like many others had been infiltrated into the thousands of genuine refugees flooding across the border to Vienna. His father was a cut-out between the Soviet Embassy in London and an important branch of the British Communist Party in the London area. The contact made by the young man with Sir Andrew Vane had not been accidental.

Viktor Gabor was a telephone operator on the International Exchange and Wednesday was one of his free days. He had made his way to Chiswick before lunch. The meeting was in one of the small Victorian terraced houses in a quiet, tree-lined, old-fashioned road just beyond the tube station at Turnham Green.

Apart from Gabor there was a woman from the teaching staff at the London School of Economics, a member of the IRA based in London, and a local councillor from a north London district. The man who acted as convener was a free-lance journalist who supplied scandal paragraphs for anyone who would pay him. His clients ranged from one of the Sundays through a wide variety of media down to the radical satirical cheap sheets.

'What are the advantages if he does live with Vane?'

The woman from the LSE spoke up rather tetchily. 'I should have thought that would be obvious, Terry. Vane is, after all the Parliamentary Secretary to the Minister. And it's the Minister who matters for us.'

'Is he going to get anything though?' This, from the IRA man.

'I think he can get anything we want but we ought to do it right away. He can't start asking things the moment he arrives.'

The journalist leaned back. 'Agreed, Gabor. But what you're all missing is the fact that he might be able to get what we want just by seeing him more often. If he goes to live with Vane then Vane could himself become suspect.'

Gabor smiled and shook his head. 'He wants the boy with him and we haven't got time now for a slow build-up.'

'OK. We'll leave it to you to arrange then, Viktor. Let me know what happens. Now Susan, what's the latest with the students?'

Nobody had asked about the boy's feelings. They were irrelevant.

When the visiting team at Villa Park score a goal, you can hear the roar all over Aston, but when the Villa score, you can hear the roar in Erdington. On the south side of Slade Road in Erdington there is a network of short roads criss-crossing the hill that leads down to Brookvale Park. When Jim Maclean was a boy he thought that Brookvale Park was about the size of Africa. Military bands played there, and draughtsmen from Kynoch's played tennis with their girl friends. Fathers rowed families at 3*d*. an hour, and small boys threw sticks for other people's dogs, and rode down the sandy slopes on rusty trays.

But Jim Maclean was no longer a small boy. The bandstand had crumbled into disuse, the tennis courts were long abandoned, and the lake itself looked like it really was – a hundred yards by five hundred. The boats were still for hire, but fathers didn't row families any more. But two areas of Brookvale Park had kept their dignity. The toilets still lurked discreetly behind the laurels and the privet, and the bowling-green was still shaved with devoted care. At least half the councillors of Birmingham City Council would have been surprised to know that the bowling-green hut was the venue for a weekly meeting of communists and fellow travellers. They would not have been horrified, merely surprised. Only illicit sex in the bowling-green hut would have provoked horror. For that matter even licit sex would have been frowned on.

When Jim Maclean was a junior draughtsman at one of the local foundries it had been his breathtaking duty at four o'clock on a Friday afternoon to check the state of the game at the big drawing office of one of the large Midland car plants. It was the car plant's habit to resist pressure for increased wages by skilful anticipation. They were tipped off a few days before a claim was to be made and on the following Friday they would sack 400 draughtsmen, tracers and designers. When this happened it had a cooling effect on drawing-office wage-claims, not only in Birmingham, but as far north as Derby and as far east as Peterborough. Just before the war started there was an application that would have brought a married draughtsman's takings to nearly £5 a week. That week, every member of the car plant's drawing-office, from chief designer to the print kid, found his wages packet a little bulkier. The bulk was provided by insurance cards and an hour's notice of dismissal.

Hector Maclean, Jim's father, was one of those men, and a month later he had hung himself in the bandstand at Brookvale Park. As his wife had said at the time, he'd always loved the music in the park.

When the war came Jim Maclean had been a conscientious objector. The Tribunal had not liked his reasons and he had done two months in an Army prison – the 'glasshouse' at Colchester. Another two months in prison as a civilian in Winson Green, and society had patted into shape a dedicated 'Bolshie'. When he had contacted the local party in 1942 they thought he was too good to carry a card. That was for the sheep and the hot-heads.

At a conservative estimate Jim Maclean had contrived and organized the loss of nine million man-days since the war. But no employer had ever heard of him, and he wasn't on the police records even for a parking offence. He had never owned a car, and never would.

That Wednesday the meeting was twenty strong. Even with men sitting on the floor others had to stand. There were men from most unions but few were officials. They represented engineering, transport, power workers, the railways, the postal services and typesetters. It's surprising how few people can bring a whole country to a stop.

The meeting was brief and Maclean's instructions were to the point. There were to be claims for a fifty per cent increase in wages and shorter hours for the two million workers that these men could control. The claim was to be put forward at all branch and plant meetings in two weeks' time. There would be a work-to-rule by the following Friday if the claim had not been agreed to. There were few questions and everyone there knew what it meant. This was the start. And it was going to be started by them – in Birmingham and the Midlands.

For civilians it is accepted that the wages of sin is death. In the Army it is accepted that the wages of sin is Catterick Camp. The best that even the shiftiest estate agent could have said for this benighted property of Her Majesty's Ministry of Defence was that it was set in the green fields of Olde England. They were green because of the almost continuous rain. Another reason why mention of the name could strike despair in the hearts of signallers, and others, doing Her Majesty's business around the world, was the paralysing isolation of the site.

One of its nearer neighbours is the town of Northallerton which encompasses about 6,000 souls, and is where the English defeated the Scots in 1138 at the Battle of the Standard. But outside this humble market town was Conby Towers, the home of a successful man named Tom Cowan. It wasn't his real name but it was what he called himself, and few knew otherwise.

Tom Cowan had made several fortunes out of selling war-surplus goods to India, Pakistan and a wide variety of lesser-known states. It was an important part of Tom's image that he had been in the Army during the war for four long years, and that he went in as a private and came out as a private. Those were his own oft-repeated words, and the world was divided into those who found the fact amazing, and those who saw it as proof that justice was sometimes done.

He was a rubicund man, red of face, outgoing and cheerful of disposition. Most people called him Uncle Tom and he loved that. Almost every night, and certainly every weekend, Conby Towers was the home from home of twenty or more soldiers from the camp. Because they were awaiting posting it meant that no group stayed the same for more than a week or two.

But Sunday nights were by invitation only. On Sundays Uncle Tom would put on a show in the big ballroom. A comedian who made jokes about officers, a folk-singer who sang of down-trodden Negroes, and a conjurer. But, delight that those were, they weren't the magnet that made the simple soldiers fawn over Uncle Tom for a Sunday invitation. It was the girls who caused that. One thing was for sure, the girls were not Northallerton girls. They were what the tabloids call 'models'. They were pretty and, as if chosen by a master hand, they all had big busts and long legs. There were never more than three or four so there was no question of a girl for every squaddie, but as in any good socialist economy it was a case of 'to each according to his needs'. Uncle Tom kept in touch with all his boys for birthdays and Christmas. Uncle Tom was a lovely man, a rough diamond admittedly, but the diamond was there all right.

On Monday mornings Uncle Tom was busy in his darkroom. He always developed the six cassettes himself, then there was no doubt that the films had been properly exposed. If 'properly' was the *mot juste*. He had once suggested to the Direktor that half-plates were big enough for the record. But the orders were two glossy 10 × 8s of every shot, with the details on the back of both. Whilst it never put Tom Cowan off sex, he did get sick of the sight of the human backside. The resolving power of the 135 mm Nikkor lens is very good, good enough to tell grain from goose-pimples.

Chapter 14

For the third week in October it was good weather by Moscow standards. There was frost on the ground but blue sky above. There had been a flurry of snow in the night and some of it still clung to the front of the large, ornate building that filled one side of Dzerzhinsky Square. The building was the Moscow headquarters of the KGB, known as the Centre to its alumni.

Boris Yasnov's office was at the back of the big building where a recent budget had allowed a flurry of modernization. The computer installation had been air-conditioned at last and there were forty new offices that even IBM executives would have found acceptable. The meeting was to be in the old conference room and Yasnov carried the two boxes of documents down the corridor and through to the front of the building. He had had a new suit run up in London. It was a soft, light-weight, blue mohair by Dormeuil, and he felt good in it.

There were two KGB lieutenants laying out the places at the big oval table and spread down the centre were ashtrays, bowls of fruit, glasses and jugs of spa-water. At the head of the table was a bowl of turkish delight. For the sole use of the chairman. With a chairman like Marshal of the Soviet Union Klimenty Yefremovich Voroshilov, nobody had any doubt where he stood. He may be long in the tooth, but as an erstwhile President-Chairman of the Presidium of the Supreme Soviet of the USSR, and the man who shoved out Kruschev, he knew the ropes.

The meeting started half an hour later, and with no preamble the Marshal set off.

'I've been looking at this subversion operation in Britain and it seems to me there are a lot of loose ends. The total plan against the Americans as worked out in the Special Collection is clear and precise, but this operation against the British doesn't seem to have a beginning or an end. So somebody had better tell me where I'm wrong. You're in charge Yasnov – explain.'

Yasnov had not expected to be called on so early in the meeting and he reached forward to stub out his cigarette in the ashtray. The old boy was in one of his fake stupid moods and those were always pretty dangerous. But he took a deep breath and launched into his piece without being too sure where he was heading.

'Well sir, it's true that the parameters of this operation have . . .' The Marshal butted in.

'For God's sake, Yasnov, don't use those bloody silly words. Parameter – sounds like a drop-out from the university. Maybe you need . . . ah well, get on with it.'

'Sorry sir. What we are aiming at is creating a situation in Britain where the workers are demanding proper pay and working conditions. They are refused by the Government and this causes the type of unrest that leads to open disorders on a scale that can justify the workers appealing for help from the Soviets.'

He leaned back hoping that someone else would pick up the ball. But nobody did. The Marshal was chewing turkish delight and looking up at the chandelier. After a few moments' silence he looked across at Yasnov.

'Yasnov, that sounds like a bloody press release from those smart buggers in the Ministry of Information.' He banged his fist on the table. 'I don't want your cover story. I want to know what you're actually going to do.'

General Kurochkin was head of the Frunze Military Academy and he was too good and too old to be impressed by fists banging on tables.

'I think, comrade Marshal, that Yasnov is much concerned at the moment with his cover story. It's not important in this room but it's of prime importance in Britain.'

Voroshilov smiled a grim smile at the General as he looked at him. Then he turned back to Yasnov.

'Carry on, comrade.'

'We have three networks in Britain. Two are "illegals" controlled from Paris and Dublin and one is a "legal" controlled from the Dublin Embassy. They have not been there long enough to be really experienced but they are co-ordinating the two "illegal" networks very successfully. Government policy in London is to control inflation at all costs, so it is our objective to generate high wage claims. The unions have always made the mistake of getting a claim settled by a big union and then the others take their turn. They call it "leapfrogging". The Press and Government have been making a big thing of being anti-leap-frogging. So we have recommended that all the claims are at least a twenty-five per cent increase with shorter working hours. And all the claims go in together, with a short deadline. The employers and the Government will have to refuse and then there's a complete stoppage. A possible general strike again. There'll be tough picketing leading to pitched battles with the police and the Army, and a breakdown of all organized government.'

Voroshilov looked around the table, his tongue probing his teeth. He finally came back to Yasnov.

'I'm sure you understand, comrade, that what you've described won't happen that way. These sorts of things are always untidy. How many experienced people have you got on the job?'

'Over two hundred KGB. Fifty-seven GRU. Our embassies in Paris, London and Dublin, and the Polish, Czech and Hungarians in London. But they are not informed on the relationship with the Special Collection.'

'What's Pyatokov's view on all this?'

'He's played a major part in the planning. He thinks it will work provided we keep the pressure on.'

Voroshilov was slowly rubbing his jaw. The old war-horse was thinking. He was nodding his head as if agreeing with something that had been said. But no one had spoken. Then he reached for another cube of turkish delight, and before putting it in his mouth he said, 'Now there's one more thing. There was a report came to me last week from the GRU that large-scale maps of the Soviet Union were at the Pentagon and probably in Paris and London too. There was some vague story that they leaked through the KGB. You know anything about this?'

'It's not in my official area, sir. Maybe you'd rather have an authoritative statement.'

Voroshilov's little piggy eyes looked at him shrewdly. 'Maybe I would. But you tell me.'

'The cartographic section of the GRU worked in conjunction

with the KGB and maps were produced that were substantially distorted. Distances, contours, river lines, names, were all shifted or altered so that they were useless.'

'But they'll have their own maps from the satellites.'

'Not with names, sir. It's just a confusion tactic. The maps were leaked through the KGB.'

Voroshilov nodded. The nearest he ever came to overt approval.

'Well we'll take your detailed report on the subversion operation after lunch.' He looked at an old-fashioned watch from his tunic pocket.

'We'll assemble again at one o'clock.'

Semichastny's office in the Moscow Centre was big and old-fashioned. The tall windows gave little light because of the heavy curtains, and the beautiful lamp on the ornate desk gave an exaggerated chiaroscuro to the faces of the two men at the desk. There was a tray with sandwiches – trout, smoked salmon and beetroot. A silver spoon with a deep scoop lay on a heaped bowl of caviar. A basket was filled with bread, from poppy-seed rolls to the grey Minsk pistolets that were the Marshal's favourites. Gideon would have chosen Voroshilov for his band of warriors because he drank his chicken broth without the aid of a spoon and as if there was nothing to food but to get it down. He threw back his head for the last dregs and the big cup rattled back on to its saucer. As he drew the back of his hand across his mouth he said, 'I gather Yasnov is not yet in the picture, Semichastny.'

'I thought it best to have one more meeting in the old style, Marshal. He will be along soon and we'll put him straight. This afternoon's meeting can show a consensus for going back to the drawing board. But I want to leave the subversion operation with top priority. Nobody can object to that and it gives Yasnov all the scope he'll need.' He smiled across at the old Marshal. 'You handled it very well this morning, comrade.'

'You were listening?'

Semichastny nodded, and then put his finger on one of a row of buttons and leaned back.

'I'll get Yasnov in.'

.   .   .   .   .

95

Yasnov's desk was modern teak, a straight copy from a range of Danish office equipment. He sat back in the comfortable chair, idly stirring his coffee. The strategy for the afternoon meeting had been laid down by Semichastny so there were no snags there. Just the one little problem. The KGB and the Red Army were going it alone, ignoring the Presidium. All Semichastny's waffle couldn't disguise that. And Semichastny was obviously inviting him on to the bandwagon. So the problem was the question of the Presidium. Was there any mileage in tipping them off? Experience said that tippers-off always got their hands caught in the machinery. Semichastny would have already worked out the likelihood of his blowing the gaff to the Party boys and if he reckoned it was unlikely, it would be because he couldn't see a reward for Yasnov in playing the informer. He closed his eyes and rested his head on the back of the chair. The Presidium would tolerate the subversion but not the follow-on strike against the Americans. The KGB and the Army were ostensibly following out orders. Keeping the subversion going as a major operation and standing down the American bit to 'planning only' level. But when the subversion plan worked it wouldn't take more than four or five days to take the wrappers off the US strike plan. It took him two minutes to decide what to do. He opted for climbing on the bandwagon. No part of his thinking concerned the wisdom or otherwise of what the KGB and the Red Army were up to, or what its consequences might be for Russia.

One thing it certainly would mean was frequent trips to London, and he instinctively touched his ribs. Even through the silk shirt he could feel the marks.

Chapter 15

There was a working table in Felinski's quarters and he had sat there almost continuously for nine hours. He had read the dossiers on Leggat and the CIA. He had also read the file on Maxwell. It was clear that Maxwell was an expert operator with an outstanding record. Then there had been the long slog through all the dossiers on every member of the staff at the London embassies of the Soviet Union, Poland, Czechoslovakia and Hungary.

In a small room off the main room was a Security Signals captain with a range of equipment that covered two walls. There were three transmitters, half a dozen receivers and the remote controls for two directional aerials. There was a VDU and a keyboard terminal linked into Central Records.

Just before midnight Felinski had eaten, but although he was tired his mind could not stop churning over the hundreds of pieces of the jigsaw. He had a key now to the white door in Curzon Street and as he came into the street he turned and walked slowly up to the corner of Park Lane. The traffic at midnight was almost as heavy as midday. A party was leaving the Playboy Club and Felinski obliquely thought of the girl. And with some sudden inexplicable reflex he turned and walked back to the corner beyond the white door. The Curzon Cinema looked almost the same as it had those many years ago, but in an odd sort of way the passed time didn't make him feel old. There were photographs of a lovely blonde in the display frames and he recognized Catharine Deneuve. It was a revival of Bunuel's *Belle de Jour*. As he looked only half-consciously at the photographs, a voice said quietly and with a heavy accent, 'Die Brücke ist kaput', and as he turned, a hand clamped on his arm. Voronov was smiling and he changed to Russian. 'I just checked in with Maxwell.'

'Where are you staying?'

'Same place as you, there's another suite for me. Maxwell's

staying at the American Embassy. He'll be over tomorrow. Said he'd had enough for today so I came alone.'

'How'd you come over?'

'Scheduled flight, a 747.'

'I've sent a contact message to Leggat.'

'Which drop did you use?'

'Gorky Park.'

They walked back slowly together and as they sat with a whisky, Felinski said, 'I've worked out a way to get him out.'

'Tell me.'

'Not until I've slept on it. Any reason why you shouldn't come to Berlin with me?'

Voronov grinned. 'Hundreds of reasons. But I'll come, comrade.'

Felinski was standing up pouring out another whisky into the two glasses when Voronov spoke again. 'How much money they pay you for this, Steve?'

'None. How much are they paying you?'

'I get a regular salary from CIA but for this job I get extra. Another fifty thousand dollars to get Leggat out. And now I get plenty more if we stop this operation in Britain.'

'How much did you get in the KGB?'

'Peanuts. Those bastards pay me ten thousand roubles a year and my expenses. If I was a foreigner I would get ten times as much.' Voronov yawned, stretched his arms slowly and stood up. 'Your people say no girls allowed to come here.'

Felinski smiled and sipped his whisky. 'They'll fix you up, Kliment. I'll speak to them tomorrow. It's too late now, anyway you must be tired out.'

'They already fixed a place. A flat in Ebury Street. I'll take a little walk, comrade. I'll need your key.'

As he came out of the Panaletskaya underground station, Leggat waited for a gap in the traffic that flowed down Valovaya Street. After he had crossed he looked back to the underground station, but nobody was watching him. He passed the statue of Dobrynin and the derelict homes behind Oktober Square. At the far side of the square was the entrance to the Oktober Square underground station. It was much nearer to

98

the Park of Culture and Rest than the Panaletskaya, but he could see the militia men standing in pairs. As usual they were keeping an eye on the foreigners staying at the Warsaw Hotel.

Leggat walked briskly over the Crimea Bridge which spans the Sadovaya as it flows steadily to join the Moskva River. On the massive architrave of the gigantic stone porch at the entrance to Gorky Park, the hammer and sickle emblems were white with pigeon droppings, and at the foot of the porch was the old lady who sometimes had her basket against the Kremlin walls. For one moment he feared she might recognize him but she was busy serving a group of workmen with caviar sandwiches. He strolled across the low hilly ground that borders the Moskva River and then walked to the Pushkin Embankment and watched the ferry boat tying up at the landing stage. Finally he arrived at Neskuchny Gardens, and counting carefully he came to the third green bench. There was nobody sitting on any of the elegant, green-painted benches, and as he approached the third bench he stopped and looked down at his shoe. He made to bend and then turned to the bench and sat down, leaning over to tie his shoe-lace. As he straightened up he fastened his coat-collar against the wind and gazed around the garden at the banks of Michaelmas daisies and chrysanthemums. As he looked, his fingers curved along the underside of the narrow wooden slats that gave the bench its shape and comfort. Where they passed through the first of the cast-iron supports he felt it. His fingers closed over the small metal circle and pulled. The light magnet still held and he pushed it sideways till it fell into his palm. His hand went in his pocket as he stood up, stamped his feet, and walked back to the bridge.

On Leggat's desk was a foolscap sheet in single-spaced typing. There was a list of questions from Yasnov.

1. We have a report that high-rise building called Centre Point is part of secret government tunnel system to be used in post-nuclear bomb situation. Normal procedure for large new buildings is for plans to be submitted to Fine Arts Commission. This not done for Centre Point. Additionally, building has been subject of much political criticism by both political parties but neither party has taken action. Comments please.

2. What is connection between GPO micro-wave towers at

Stokenchurch and Bagshot? Reports indicate this is part of emergency control system.

3. Suggest source for details of 'D' notices in last six months.

4. See 'P' file on VORONOV, Kliment, and attached 'Known associate' file FELINSKI, Stephen. Felinski appears to be an officer in Security Service. Have you personal knowledge of this subject?

5. See attached updated file 97419 – 'An appreciation of Irish Republic Security Services'. Your comments on conflicting views of KGB and Dublin Embassy.

6. Your comments on attached file covering ETU, TGWU and AEU. Particular emphasis on alleged penetration by Special Branch and MI5. Which Minister would be responsible for authorizing this?

7. Can you identify the subjects photographed in attached file marked '87 Curzon Street'?

Felinski had spent an hour with Tim MacNay and two senior men from Special Branch. Felinski had picked out seven of the staff of the Soviet Embassy in London for full-time surveillance. This was going to take eighteen experienced men and had caused some protests from Special Branch itself. The protests had been overruled by Clayton, and Felinski had again been assured that he had top priority for all the services he might need.

The meeting with Voronov and Maxwell was going to be tricky because of Leggat's background. But Felinski needed and wanted CIA co-operation and he was determined to play it down the middle no matter what embarrassment it caused in government circles in London. Only the PM, the Home Secretary and the Leader of the Opposition had been told of Leggat's real background.

'Bill, before we get down to planning there's an item I want to raise with you. But before I do I want to know how many people are informed about your liaison with SIS.'

'The head of CIA and the Chief of European Operations. Say five or six people in all.'

'And who do they tell?'

'Maybe nobody. Depends on the nature of the information.'

'What was your people's reaction to the fact that Leggat isn't English but Russian?'

Maxwell smiled. 'Critical of your security but technically sympathetic.'

'What about using him?'

Maxwell shook his head. 'No way, Steve. We have a policy about turned agents. One turn we'll go with. More we won't touch. It's never worked. We've tried it.'

'And if I go along with Leggat?'

'Let him come over, you mean?'

'Yes. And use him of course.'

'Then I would have to tell my people and I've no doubt it would go to the White House in the hour. And I've no doubt they'd clamp down.'

'You mean they would withdraw you?'

'No, I don't think they'd do that. This is too important for that, but I think there would be areas of co-operation that would be withdrawn. They'd probably monitor the operation. Me as well.'

'What if we go on using Leggat for information but don't pull him out?'

'That would be OK, but I'd suggest we give it heavy checking before we build on it.'

'We should do that anyway. But leaving him in Moscow isn't what he wants and he may not co-operate on that basis. What do you think, Kliment?'

Voronov grinned. 'Well as an ex-KGB boy I don't trust anyone. So for me I guess if this was a KGB operation we should get Leggat out and then give him the treatment.'

'Well for the moment let's leave it that we do intend bringing out Leggat because we have to, and go on using him as a prime source. Does that leave you OK, Bill?'

'I guess so. Let's see what happens.'

'Now I want to go back a bit and I want your views, Kliment. When did the Soviets decide on this first-strike gambit against the Americans?'

'That followed on from Kruschev's time. The General Staff were strongly against the Kruschev adventures and their opposition solidified at the time of the Cuban missiles and Kennedy. It wasn't Kennedy whom Kruschev backed down from; he backed down from the General Staff who were enraged at what he was doing. He would have gone on if they hadn't

101

threatened him. Then we got the Bay of Pigs and the General Staff had done an appreciation of Kennedy's likely case. It was taken for granted the Americans would claim that they were entitled to support the Cuban dissidents just as the Soviets supported their people in Hungary. The Americans didn't use this argument, they behaved as if they were the guilty parties. Someone at Frunze did an analysis of American attitudes and military thinking and that was really the start of this operation.'

'When was that?'

'It's difficult to be precise. Somewhere between 1960 and 1962.'

'And what were the conclusions of the analysis?'

'The conclusion was that the Americans lacked the ability to work out an effective nuclear strategy. They were doing with nuclear war-heads what the West had done with tanks and aircraft. They were absorbing them as weapons into their existing arms of service.'

'Who did this report?'

'The first report was by Colonel-General Gastilovich and it became the basis of the Special Collection.'

'Why did they conclude that the Americans couldn't work out an effective nuclear strategy?'

'Ah yes. Well let us take the production of weapons. The Americans spend millions of dollars on making their weapons "clean". Minimum radioactive contamination. The Soviets are criticized because they are behind in technology, their weapons still being dirty. Now do you get it?'

Felinski shook his head. Voronov continued.

'Well this is exactly what Gastilovich said was the fundamental thing. The actual practical difference between Western philosophy and Marxist philosophy. I'm not a military man, comrades, but what the Colonel-General was saying is that the Americans are planning and designing their nuclear war-heads to do their damage by explosion, or impact. But the Soviets think that "dirty" war-heads with maximum radioactive contamination of terrain will be a principal factor of combat. Do you see the argument now, Steve?'

'Yes, I do. The Soviets want to paralyse large areas, not just specific targets.'

'Well that's the basis on which they plan this attack. Plus one

102

more. It is known that without doubt the Soviet Union could not sustain a long major war. The country's economy and the people's morale would not endure a long ordeal. It is now an accepted fact in Soviet thinking that war with the capitalists is inevitable. That they have to strike first follows naturally. It would have come before if Kruschev had had his way.'

'And the operation against this country?'

'To neutralize it. And to neutralize Europe. That is all.'

'Who is controlling this operation in Moscow?'

'All the indications are that it's Yasnov.'

'Well we've got to cover these networks. They all operate in this country but it looks as if at least two of them are controlled from outside. One from Paris and one from Dublin. Any views on how we divide our time?'

Maxwell was used to politicians and he came back quickly, 'That's up to you, Steve, you're the boss. Your people will expect you to co-ordinate. Apart from anything else, if either Kliment or I start snooping around in this country we shall be spotted in no time.'

'What I had in mind was individual tasks. Kliment, I'd like you to go through our files on the Soviet embassies here and in Paris and Dublin. Pick out the likely controllers. I'll try to get this out of Leggat. Bill, I'd like you to get alongside Lomax at Special Branch. Go over with him all identified subversives, look at their routine weekly reports on militants and agitators and see if you can get a pattern. Let's meet tonight. Here at eight. I'll get them to lay on some food.'

There was a pile of reports and messages on Felinski's desk and he knew from experience that it was this flow of detailed information that made any counter-intelligence operation pay off. Already Leggat had given two names. One of these he passed to Voronov. He wondered why Leggat was asking for last year's 'D' notice details and asked the Moscow Embassy to supply them immediately.

Maxwell was not back till 8.15 and they finished eating an hour later. It was Maxwell who started the ball rolling.

'Steve, it's my turn to lay it on the line. How much do you know about NSA?'

'Your monitoring outfit at Fort George Meade?'

'Yep. That's the one.'

'I know pretty well what they do. Monitoring and code-breaking.'

'You know we do this on our allies as well as our enemies?'

'Taken for granted.'

'OK. They passed a monitor report to CIA today and they passed it to me. They're monitoring stuff between you and your Moscow Embassy and they've latched on to your message from Leggat and your replies. They mentioned 'D' notices.'

'Any comments from them?'

'No, but I thought you ought to know.'

'Anything from Special Branch?'

'Yes. There's at least one pattern. The Birmingham area's got a lot going at the moment. I've pulled it into a file and there are some boys to have a closer look at.'

Felinski turned to Voronov. 'What about the embassies?'

'In Paris I can tell you OK but I can also tell you that that network is number two. At least it's not number one. Number one is Dublin, there are three top guys there. A political organizer, a communications man and a GRU fellow who's their best guerrilla warfare man. He's been in Ireland for two years helping the IRA before they had a Soviet Embassy in Dublin. He was part of the Soviet permanent trade mission in the Republic. If we tail them we'll begin to get a picture.'

Chapter 16

It had taken Leggat almost fifteen minutes to clear himself through the routine security network of the Lubyanka. He stood at the top of the steps and looked out over the square. It was a fine cold night with a deep blue sky and stars so bright that it looked like a stage set. He glanced at his watch. There was time to walk. Tonight was a special night at the Bolshoi, they were going all nostalgic and dancing Gliere's 'The Red Poppy'. All Moscow felt a warm glow for Gliere. Prokoviev's first teacher. And 'The Red Poppy' was Moscow's tribute.

He was ahead of time when he got to Sverdlov Square and he stood for a few moments. It was his favourite square, the gayest and liveliest square in Moscow. They'd put lights over Vitali's pretty fountain, and on the other side the bust of Karl Marx jutted out from its granite block.

There was a hard frost on the square when he came out after the performance and he made his way carefully to the restaurant in the Metropole. Back at his apartment after the meal he poured out a brandy and put on the light at his small but ornate writing desk. It was indeterminate French but in the style of Louis Quinze with china inkwells and a long concave recess for pens and pencils. He made himself comfortable in his chair and reached carefully for the slim fluted leg that supported the desk on its base. A slight turn and a click, and he reached under the desk and felt in the secret compartment for the book. He laid it on the desk top and admired the leather binding. It was Leggat's insurance, his source of capital in a capitalist world. In his own shorthand he had amassed 150,000 words for his autobiography. Just the American and British rights would keep him in happy affluence for the rest of his life. He had not been able to make the final decision between a smallish château on the Loire or something more elaborate in Ireland. Maybe he'd have both. He wrote another five hundred words before he retired to bed.

.   .   .   .   .

It had taken two days for Felinski and Voronov to work out alternative routes for Leggat's flight and it had finally rested between two possibles. The first entailed a visit to Warsaw on the excuse of co-operation with the Polish secret police, Z-11. Then the long journey by train and car to Magdeburg. At Magdeburg there was a line-crossing group who could bring Leggat over the border, just below the checkpoint at Helmstedt. The alternative was straight down the middle. Starting after duty hours on a Friday, a scheduled Aeroflot flight from Moscow to Berlin, then through the secondary checkpoint at Sonnen Allee using his red KGB identity document. All it took was confidence and arrogance. It was a few hours instead of three days, and there were a dozen cover stories for Berlin. But on the other route, once Leggat left Warsaw there was no cover story that would really hold. The message was passed back to Leggat on the Monday drop under the bench in Gorky Park. He passed his agreement back that evening in a coded telephone message to a number in Leningrad.

Leggat was taking one of the Bolshoi ballerinas to the circus and when he picked her up at the National he phoned for an official car. It was already 6.15, and the circus started in fifteen minutes. It was only 8.30 when the audience was applauding the last act, the girl on the high trapeze, with the big black eagle. He'd taken his guest back to the apartment and they had eaten the cold meats and fruit that the old 'babcha' who did his cleaning had left on the oval table.

He looked across at the girl. She was petite with big brown eyes and a slender neck. Nadia Yelena Yakolevna. He wondered why all ballerinas seemed to be called Nadia, but it made it easier to fumble their names. She was brand new, perhaps not quite untouched by human hand, but she hadn't gone the rounds of the generals; they were getting their young girls from the nurses' training college. But although Leggat could pick and choose he generally kept to ballet girls, he had a vague theory that the exercise made them better in bed. They were seldom well endowed in their busts but their neat young bottoms were always something special. She'd smiled when she sat on his lap and as his hand explored up her skirt she had finished the red caviar from the silver plate. When things went further she'd begged to take off her black velvet skirt. It was the only good one she had, but she settled back on his lap immediately after and wriggled obligingly as he put the fifty-rouble note in her small petit-point purse. He had put the full-length 'Swan Lake' on the player, and he was slightly shocked that she sat drinking her wine and listening intently to the lush music as he enjoyed her. And when it was all over she didn't appear to have noticed. After more wine he'd taken her to his bedroom and the third time he had her she was already asleep. But he knew he'd done well. He might have grey hair but there was a wonderful youthful wave to it.

He walked across into the main room. Tired, but not sleepy. He hadn't written in his diary for four days and he switched on the small pink light and sat carefully in the chair. He went automatically through the routine with the slender fluted leg, the click was so loud he wondered if the girl would awaken. He reached carefully under the desk to the secret recess and his fingers touched wood. Then as his heart pounded he moved his hand till it had touched the back and the two sides. The diary had gone. The recess was empty. He heard himself groan out loud. He was panting as he rushed to the hanging cupboard for his torch. He knelt and shone the faint light into the recess. It was empty. Perhaps, he thought, he had not put it back in its secret place. But he knew all too well that that was not possible. He searched the drawers and the desk top in vain. His breath was coming in great gulps through his open mouth. He shivered as he cried out in terror and despair. When did it go, and who had got it? But he knew all too well. Maybe they wouldn't be able to decipher his shorthand. But he knew that hope was futile too. Maybe they had not yet deciphered it, maybe there was still time. He felt cold and he was shivering violently. But the adrenalin coursing through his blood gave him the courage he needed. He'd try. He'd try and see what happened.

He dressed quickly and quietly and slipped his KGB card into his wallet and his passport into his coat pocket. In the street his car was still there and nobody moved. The car started easily and he glanced at his wrist-watch. There was an early plane at 6.15 and he turned the car northwards and drove carefully towards the airport. If he judged the timing well he'd arrive with only

107

fifteen minutes to spare. Then he saw the two men in the faint dawn light. They were uniformed militia and one was waving him down with a torch. He was tempted to bash his way through but he guessed that that would be fatal, and he pulled up. The taller one rapped on the window and he let it down slowly.

'Where are you going, comrade?'

'To the airport.'

'Show me your Moscow resident pass, comrade.'

He took out the red KGB book and the militia man saluted. He checked the photo and the description, and handed it back.

'Sorry to hold you up, gospodin.'

And they both saluted and stood to one side.

There was a swirl of snow as Leggat swung the car into the airport car-park. There were ten places for VIP cars and Leggat placed his car carefully in one of the centre slots. As he walked through the main doors he saw that the flight had been called and people were queueing at the far gate. The KGB red folder was good for any internal travel in the Soviet Union and Warsaw Pact countries, and he was waved through without any formalities. And then there was a good omen. A junior KGB officer came out of the KGB office and, noticing him, nodded and smiled. For a moment he wondered if he had made a foolish mistake and that the diary was still there, but he knew there had been no mistake. But they obviously were not looking for him or he'd never have got this far.

There were no drinks or food on the early morning flight, but the stewardess gave out vouchers for a meal at the Berlin terminal. He was waiting silently, afraid of the cockpit door opening and one of the crew coming back. The Centre could radio-contact the plane all the way to touch-down. They were landing at the Schönefeld airfield and most of the passengers would be continuing the flight to Dresden and Prague.

The snow was two inches thick at Berlin and only three other passengers crunched their way to the small terminal buildings. The others moved across to the small queue waiting for the restaurant to open. Leggat walked through to the exit. There was a short line of taxis but he walked past them and down the long road that led to the checkpoint. The snow was falling slowly and in the silence his confidence had returned. He was halfway to the checkpoint when the plane turned overhead and flew south. As he looked ahead he saw the checkpoint buildings just in front of the wall. There were two white and black painted poles each side of the checkpoint offices and guardroom. Two Grenzpolizei were at the first pole and they checked his KGB pass carefully and handed it back. The pole swung up and Leggat walked forward. He half smiled because he knew he'd made it. With ten steps he would be past the second pole and then with a couple of strides he would be across the white line that marked the border with West Berlin. As he reached the second barrier he waited for it to rise, and turned smiling to the guards. And then he saw him. Yasnov was leaning carelessly against the door of the guardroom. As he walked towards Leggat he nodded to the guards, who raised their guns. He stood a couple of feet from Leggat and looked him in the face. 'Kakvy dayekhaly, Leggat?'

Yasnov made no move to break Leggat's fall as he collapsed. The two guards lifted the unconscious body and Yasnov picked up the red identity card from the snow.

Chapter 17

Almost any capital city in the world has a unity, a coming-together that allows identity; some to a peak of 'charisma', some to a point of despair. Dublin, as in everything else, is the unique exception. If there *are* leprechauns in Ireland then they're not in Dublin, for Dublin has ghosts, and in Dublin the people feed the ghosts. No poverty, no peace, has ever stopped that. At that Easter when the brutal lover was flung back across the Irish Sea he left his bastard stamp along with his alimony. If you want to find the Irish-lovers, then look in England. And if you want to tear down the English, then do your recruiting in Ireland.

If you want to understand the Top People of Dublin, then start with Proust; for bigotry and wit, poetry and vulgarity, neurosis and passion are theirs. The Irish got the ruling class they deserved, but they had the wisdom to create the Pale anew and confine them to Dublin. And there they sport and feud, shock and contrive, charm and beguile, to their hearts' content. And in Kerry, Cork and Limerick they don't mean a thing. The writers, the artists, flee to England, Guinness in hand, to earn a living. And their English equivalents fly to Ireland for Charlie Haughey's tax remissions. Everyone's happy and everyone's sad. No doubt the Irish are God-fearing, and no doubt the feeling's reciprocated.

To the immediate north of Dublin city, Howth Head dominates the arm of Dublin Bay. Almost two miles from the harbour itself the road seems to peter out and where it starts to falter there is a well-kept track to a farm-house and a group of buildings that are signposted as O'Malley's Farm.

Grainne van Rijk had inherited the farm and the land when her father died in 1944. She'd been almost ten years old. Her father had died in the attack on Nijmegen. He was an officer in the Parachute Brigade. He had hated the Germans even more than the English, and the small girl had inherited that too. It was nearly twelve years after her father's death that she had met Jan van Rijk.

Some countries' fighting didn't end in 1945, and Holland was one of them. Van Rijk had been a paratroop sergeant in the Dutch East Indies and had a smashed knee to prove it. He'd chosen to finish his education at Trinity College and it was there that he'd met Grainne O'Malley. It was the first time he'd seen black, black hair coupled with clear green eyes, or at least he thought it was. She wasn't a student, she'd come with a friend to a Saturday night 'hop', and with a directness that was inherent in her genes she'd asked the young man who never danced, for the pleasure of a waltz. He'd smiled a friendly enough smile and had explained about his knee and turned at the bar to buy her a drink. As he turned back to ask what it should be, he'd seen the tears in the big green eyes, and his smile had slowly faded.

He'd courted her for a year and he'd never done more than kiss her. He never attempted more and he was happy. He went to London when his lust was too great. They had married at the church in Malahide because that was the church where she had been baptized.

Van Rijk had taken over all the farm-work and there was a man and a girl to help him. It was early in 1968 when he first realized how much his lovely wife hated the English. She'd been telling him about Erskine Childers landing the rifles at Howth harbour and he'd noticed the emphasis on Maud Gonne, the Englishwoman who had teased the Irishmen in her campaign for the Irish. He had not been surprised when three months later he had found the rifles in the barn. They were Armalite AR-18s without magazines. While they were eating that evening he had spoken about them.

'The things in the big barn, Grainne darling. They've got gas pistons and they'll rust in two days in there.'

She smiled back at him.

'First you teach a farmer's daughter how to farm, and now you're going to teach an Irish girl about guns.'

He got on with his food and without looking up he said, 'I didn't see the magazines, girl, but they'll rust too.'

For four years he'd known what was going on but he didn't interfere. He watched the comings and goings and was aware of meetings and phone calls. It was when he had found the first box of Soviet Model 40 Tokarevs that he knew she was getting out of her depth. It was agreed that he would take over and the men concerned had been agreeable. Despite the stiff leg he was more a soldier than all of them.

The small barn had been converted into a workshop with spares and equipment to service anything from a Lee-Enfield to a Soviet SVD Sniper's rifle. And in the end it was van Rijk who liaised with the Russians and Poles. Within a year he was running all the action into Northern Ireland and England.

In the previous day's reports that had come from Central Intelligence to Felinski was a report from the Moscow Embassy that they had lost contact with Leggat.

There was a pile of newspaper cuttings. One in *The Times* read:

At British Steel's Llanby plant 250 production workers in the Slabbing Mill went on strike after operating a 'Go-slow' during the week. Their action coincided with a return to work by 166 other workers from the hot-strip mill who had been on strike for four days in protest over the Corporation's decision to suspend the guaranteed weekly wage agreement.

A note referred to P, File 9714.

A cutting from the *Daily Telegraph* read:

The *Daily Mirror* and the *Daily Express* lost over a million copies of their Monday editions due to industrial action. Further disruption in the publication of national newspapers is expected after today's meetings of NUJ chapels at several publishing groups.

There was a typed reference which said 'Refer you surveillance report 197819'.

A long item in the *Birmingham Post* analysed the loss of 27 per cent of production in ten months at British Leyland. There was a statement from B-L's chairman and from a shop-steward. Felinski's attention was drawn to nine surveillance reports.

There was a Security Signals report on increasing radio traffic from the Soviet embassies in Paris, London and Dublin.

. . . . .

NSA at Fort George Meade had passed a report to the CIA who had passed it to Maxwell. It indicated a high-grade code being used in the Dublin area which resembled an as yet unbroken code used between Moscow and a mobile transmitter in south-east England.

There were two reports of a Soviet submarine in the Irish Sea, and a mine-sweeper of the 'Polukhin' class had been seen without navigation lights off the Cork coast.

A lieutenant of the Black Watch leading a patrol in the Bally-conell area on the border reported seeing an unusual weapon. He had sighted it through field glasses on difficult terrain and under continuous fire from light weapons, but he was convinced it was a Russian SAM-7 missile.

At Kent and Essex universities protest meetings had turned into riots and in both cases sub-machine guns had been used. At Kent a lecturer and a canteen worker had been killed. The protest had been over a Communist second-year student who had been considered below standard by the faculty head. The Vice-Chancellor had agreed to the student being reinstated. At Essex there were no deaths. Seven teaching staff were in hospital after being beaten up, and damage to a sum of £15,000 had been done by a group of rioters. Because of the weather and the shortage of glass for broken windows, 800 students had been sent home. The riot was caused by the University inviting a Liberal MP to talk on 'Co-partnership in Industry'. In both cases the rioting students numbered fewer than two hundred. There was an incomplete list of names of those concerned. Out of eighty names, more than half appeared on both lists.

There was a Special Branch report on the death of a moderate trades union leader of the AEU. With insufficient proof, it was being treated as murder with political motives.

A Military Police report on a signals sergeant who had deserted included a statement by his wife who was convinced that he was being blackmailed. He had been on a security course at Catterick when he deserted. Burnt papers from the grate in the sergeant's

113

billet had been reconstituted and they appeared to be two 10 × 8 photographs of the sergeant in a compromising situation with a girl. They had been examined by the officer who had interviewed the wife and she was not the girl in the photographs.

There was a note for Felinski to phone an Inspector Watkins of the Vice Squad.

Voronov was supervising surveillance on the Soviet Embassy in Kensington Palace Gardens and Maxwell was still liaising with Special Branch.

Felinski met Inspector Watkins at New Scotland Yard and the Inspector had two thick files on the table alongside his desk. He patted the thicker one as if it were a much-loved pet and looked at Felinski as if to emphasize the confidentiality of what he was going to say.

'Mr Felinski, people above me have suggested I should have a word with you about one of my current investigations. I don't know what you're doing and I've been told not to ask.'

He paused to allow Felinski to reciprocate by telling him without being asked. Felinski just nodded and waited for him to continue, which he did. He patted the file again as he started.

'I've been covering a vice-ring that's based in Mayfair, Mr Felinski. It specializes in sado-masochism. Got a basement all nicely fitted out – good décor – and everything from thumb-screws to a crucifix. As you probably know, a man who wants to enjoy these kind of services has to pay a high price. So we take a special interest in these areas. It's the wealthy who patronize this place and as you know the rich have power and they're party to State secrets and commercial secrets. There are some on this woman's client list who could be of interest to you. I don't know which they are but the names and files are at your disposal.'

'I expect you've got some views on the security aspects, Inspector.'

'Not really, sir, it's not my line of country, but I've put a cross against half a dozen names. I could be quite wrong though.' And he slid both files across the desk to Felinski who opened the one nearest to him and then looked up at the Inspector and said,

'Is there any question of these people being photographed in some of these perversions?'

'Good heavens sir, yes. Some of them have files of photographs, films even, and I've got a cabinet full of such stuff, including tapes. It's all at your disposal. The other file's the main one, sir.'

Inside the cover was pinned a typewritten list of names and he looked first at those that had been marked with a cross. One was an official of the Soviet Embassy, one was a junior Minister, and four were MPs. Then Felinski read carefully down the lists. There were a hundred names to a page and there were four pages: 375 names in all. After an hour when the Inspector had been in and out of the office, Felinski pushed back his chair.

'When the names have QC by them, does that really mean they are Queen's Counsel?'

'Yes, Mr Felinski, I'm afraid it does. There's rather a lot of them, I know. Something to do with having people in the dock all day. I gather the psychiatrists call it role reversal or some such thing. Same applies to the parsons of course.'

'And what explains the Peers?'

'Oh them. Spoiled as kids and now they've got too much dough. They think everything they do is OK. They reckon they make the rules not keep 'em. Probably started with their nannies, sir.'

'Have you got separate files on them all?'

'Yes sir. Those numbers in brackets are the file numbers.'

'I'll make out a list.'

On Felinski's list there were seven MPs, three Lords, five senior civil servants, two journalists, nine diplomats of one nationality or another, a well-known broadcaster, two senior army officers and a cabinet minister. He took away photocopies of the material in their files.

He showed the files of the three Soviet diplomats to Voronov who smiled broadly as he read slowly through the details. When he had closed the last file he leaned back grinning, and Felinski said, 'Your file would raise a smile or two as well, comrade.'

Voronov shook his head smiling. 'It's not that, Steve. It's that.' And he picked up the first file and opened it. There were four photographs stapled to the first sheet. One showed a man walking in the street in bright sunshine. The second was his face slightly covered at the jaw by a wine glass. The other two showed him naked and spreadeagled, tied to ring bolts on a white wall. There were splashes of blood on the wall from the weals raised on his body from a whip. The girl holding the whip was pretty and naked. Felinski looked up at Voronov.

'All three are KGB, Steve, but this one's Yasnov.'

'Are you sure?'

'No doubt at all. Just get your people in Moscow to check Yasnov's movements at the periods in this file and you'll find that this is Yasnov. Full colonel in the KGB, hanging on the wall. My God, you could play games with this lot.'

'But he must have known the risk, doing this in London.'

'Sure it's a risk but he's driven by his sex to do it. He won't be able to do it back in Moscow. He'd never get a Soviet girl to do that in a million years.'

Felinski thought of what the Vice Squad man had said about role-reversal, and it fitted all too well.

'Does the rest of the stuff in the file fit Yasnov?'

'Yes. There's no doubt about it.'

Felinski reached for the phone and dialled Inspector Watkins's number. They gave him his home number. He was off duty. The Inspector himself answered at the second ring.

'Yes.'

'Felinski here, Inspector. I'd like to ask a couple of questions. Is that all right, or is it inconvenient?'

'That's all right sir, go ahead.'

'Are these perversions catered for in most countries?'

'Oh no, sir. That's why you get so many foreigners on the list of regulars. All those Arabs, for instance. The main centre is here in London, sir.' He sounded almost proud, as if he were helping the overseas trade balance.

'How much does it cost?'

'What for, sir?'

'Well let's say whipping.'

'Oh that's pretty standard sir. It's been five quid a lash for years.'

'And the people on the crucifix and the bolts on the wall?'

'Well that's a longish job. Say a hundred quid a day.'

'Do they pay cash?'

'Everything is cash. Cash in advance.'

'Can we identify a girl with a client?'

'Generally they stick to the same one. That wouldn't be a problem.'

Yasnov had interrogated Leggat almost non-stop for seventy hours but the shock at the checkpoint had been too much. His eyes bulged and his head lay on one side. No words would come out, and the two specialists said he would never speak or make any voluntary movement again. Yasnov insisted that they put him on the machine and the flaccid body jerked like a bundle of rags at each touch of the switch. In disgust and anger he told them to give him the injection, and he died without moving again.

Chapter 18

The plane was meeting strong head-winds and bouncing a little as it thrust towards Dublin Bay. It was making a wide, curving course from the south-east and was now low over the water. As the plane banked Yasnov looked out of the window. The coast was visible and as they passed over two boats making for shelter, the plane straightened and started its descent. Nobody could ever accuse the Bord Failte of putting on a smiling face at Dublin Airport, it was surely the dreariest terminal in all Europe.

Yasnov was using his diplomatic passport and his baggage came through without checking. It was loaded into a private car and he was driven into Dublin. He looked at the sullen skies and the mournful tatty houses. Maybe Moscow was not so bad after all. And there was Paris to look forward to on the way back. He wondered if he might even slip into London for a day.

They'd booked him in again at the Royal Hibernian. It was considered politic for holders of Soviet diplomatic passports to appear to keep themselves to obvious and public places. He signed in at the reception desk and the girl noted his passport details. She gave him that odd look that he was getting used to in Dublin. They were none of them impolite but he was treated as if he was from outer space. They were amazed that he spoke some English and they looked at his London-made clothes as if they were astonished that Russians weren't dressed in wolf skins.

He'd got one of the penthouse suites, and as a matter of routine he went over the room for nearly an hour, checking for bugs. When the girl came in to turn down the bedsheets he was sitting at the glass coffee-table with the cover off the telephone, and he was probing the circuit with a small meter. It took him half an hour to do the check and to reassemble the phone. He had laid a small diode against the speaker diaphragm and crimped the two tiny wire hooks to the diaphragm leads.

It was eight o'clock when he walked down the steps of the

Hibernian and then slowly down Dawson Street. He looked in the window of the bookshop and after a few minutes a white Cortina pulled up gently and parked. He stood on the edge of the pavement as if he were going to cross the road. Then after looking both ways up and down Dawson Street, he bent, opened the car door and got in. He was at the farm before the rain started.

The Dutchman was waiting outside the farm-house and Yasnov shook his hand. He had noticed the other cars in the enclosed yard. In the main room of the farm-house were five men and two women, one of whom he knew was the Dutchman's wife.

Voronov had phoned Felinski from a kiosk at Orly. One of the men he had been checking at the Soviet Embassy in Paris had driven another man from the Embassy to Orly. He had seen them talking in the busy main concourse and it was only then that he had realized that the second man was Yasnov. He had checked quickly on the flights to Moscow but there was nothing leaving for two hours. Then he heard the loudspeakers say, 'Passagers pour Aer-Lingus Irish numéro deux cent quatorze à Dublin sont . . .' and Yasnov had shaken hands with his companion, picked up his bag and headed for the queue for the Dublin plane. Voronov had paid a hundred new francs to see the manifest, and there was Yasnov's name.

After talking to Felinski he had booked himself on a flight to London. They had met at Heathrow and flown separately, but on the same aircraft, to Dublin. They booked in at the Shelbourne. Felinski phoned the senior SIS man in Dublin to check on Yasnov. He phoned back an hour later that he was definitely not at the Embassy. But four new faces had appeared there in the previous three days. Two had been identified and were KGB men. Thirty minutes later they had phoned him again. They had located Yasnov at the Hibernian. Yasnov had left the hotel on foot and had not returned. It was now past midnight and SIS were keeping a surveillance team on the hotel.

Yasnov had been brought back to his hotel at four in the morning, and they'd taken the number of the white Cortina. It belonged to a young girl who was the current mistress of a member of the Dail. Her father was a leading member of the

Sianad and a director of a number of important companies. The SIS file on her was coming over to Felinski in the hour.

When the file came Felinski passed the pages to Voronov as he read them. Sara Mathews was twenty-four, a graduate of University College and rabidly anti-British. Travelled frequently to London and stayed for periods varying from hours to a matter of weeks. Was suspected of being an IRA courier. There were several photographs of her and she looked lively and pretty. Her circle of friends was wide, from the higher echelons of the Irish Government to the pseudo-bohemian fringe. Her closest friend was a woman – Grainne van Rijk, who owned a farm near Howth. There was a long list of names and addresses of people with whom she had frequent contact.

Felinski had sent a coded signal via the British Embassy in Dublin to get Maxwell across as quickly as possible. It was obvious that the control of Yasnov was going to keep them in Dublin for some days.

An RAF reconnaissance helicopter was blown off course a few hours later and as it checked its bearings with Traffic Control at Dublin Airport good photographs were obtained of the area of O'Malley's Farm. Felinski got them later that day by courier from Belfast.

Felinski had had an instinct that Maxwell would be able to look at the pattern of subversion in Special Branch records with a clearer eye for being an outsider. And Maxwell's report was thorough and extensive. He had picked out seventeen people whose background and records indicated a leadership role in subversive areas. Their activities over a period of two weeks had been plotted on a massive map of the country. They had used ordinary coloured map pins and coloured nylon threads, and out of the cobweb that Maxwell and two assistants had created on the map, it was clear that the operations were inter-linked and co-ordinated. One name had been struck from the list and from the tangled web two others were added and the eighteen people had been under 24-hour surveillance for five days covering a weekend. Every movement, contact, phone-call, caller and called, was monitored, and there was now a list of over two hundred involved people! There were a further one hundred and fifty who were involved but probably unaware of either their involvement or the nature of it. The CIA in London had seconded eleven men to the operation. An analysis of the situation indicated increasing activity. The Soviet net covered Post Office workers, servicemen, the trades unions, printers, docks officials and dock workers, broadcasters and power workers. There was no area in the basic life of Britain that was not included. Maxwell's estimate was that it was the culmination of at least ten years' grafting by the KGB. The other fact of major significance was the number of Irish names on the list. There were the names of five KGB officers controlling the operation. Two were on the Soviet Embassy staff in London. The other three had not been located. Nine locations had been put under electronic surveillance, three under continuous surveillance, and an attempt was being made by Special Branch men to penetrate three groups.

Felinski had made two attempts at reconnaissance of O'Malley's Farm but its isolation made it almost impenetrable to overt observation. There were no near-by buildings or houses that could be rented or bought and there was a pair of German Shepherds who kept effective guard near the entrance to the farm-buildings. The aerial photographs showed that the surrounding land gave little or no cover. A separate reconnaissance by the SIS team had confirmed the farm's impenetrability. The SIS team had kept a rough and ready surveillance. They had photographed vehicles and callers but there was little progress made. They had reported that Mrs van Rijk had looked at their car suspiciously when she was exercising a horse and had come on them as they were turning the car near the farm entrance.

The British Embassy in Moscow had reported a rumour that Leggat had died under interrogation by the KGB.

The transcript of Leggat's diary was still in the pile of papers on Yasnov's desk awaiting his return.

Felinski, Voronov and Maxwell had read through all the reports sent over from London and the reports from SIS Dublin. It was Maxwell who broke the silence as they sat around the table.

121

'We're not going to penetrate O'Malley's Farm without alarming them, Steve. Even if we do a physical penetration at night we're not going to learn much. Maybe some arms but that won't help us. These people are organizers and our only hope is to tap the phones and bug the place.'

Felinski nodded. 'What's your feeling, Kliment?'

Voronov shrugged. 'I've no doubt what we do, comrades. We squeeze Yasnov with those photographs.'

'Threaten that we'll send them to Moscow?'

'That's it, comrade.'

'What would Moscow's reaction be?'

'They'd go mad. They'd put him straight in the mincer.'

'Why should they? He can't be the only pervert in the KGB.'

'Oh for God's sake, Steve. Drink's OK. Women are OK. Even boys are OK. As long as they don't get mixed up in your work, that is. But this sort of stuff, never. They'd put him straight in the machine. In their own peculiar way they're puritans. I've told you already, you'd never get this sort of thing in the Soviet Union.' He laughed. 'Outside the Faculty of Psychology at Leningrad they've probably never even heard of such things.'

'How about if Yasnov claims that the pictures are faked?' said Maxwell.

Felinski said, 'I'd have to go back to London first and check if there is more material. What we saw may be just reference material.'

Maxwell still probed. 'What have you got in mind if we've got more stuff on Yasnov, Kliment?'

'Steve and I call on him. Show him the stuff and carry on from there.'

'What if he bluffs it out?'

'He won't. He can't. He knows what the boys in Moscow would do.'

'And what do we want from him?'

'We want the whole operation, names, plans, contacts, codes and all the rest of it.'

'OK. Say we get it and we wrap it up. Won't they just start again?'

Voronov nodded. 'They could, but there isn't time. They'd

have to put the whole thing back including the main part, the pre-emptive attack on the States.'

Maxwell said quickly, 'That could make it worthwhile. Any delay gives us time to try and work something out.'

Felinski looked at Maxwell. 'So you're for it, Bill?'

'Yes. Otherwise it's going to take months for us to penetrate all these groups.'

Felinski had phoned Inspector Watkins and took the next plane to London. At New Scotland Yard Watkins had laid out on a long table photographs, films and reels of tape. It was like an obscene harvest festival.

There were photographs in black and white and others in colour. There were photographs of Yasnov spreadeagled to the wall and others where he hung on a crucifix. Felinski looked at one which showed Yasnov with his back arched in pain and his head thrown back in ecstasy. There were others so repellent that it was an effort to look at them. The same girl appeared in all of them. Felinski, like many others, had always agreed with the media that obscenity was hard to define. This was obscenity. He actually needed to sit down.

Watkins seemed ill at ease as he looked at Felinski's pale face. 'Maybe we'd better leave the films, sir. They're much the same as this stuff. I'm afraid I've got used to it by now, sir.'

Felinski looked up at him, this ordinary-looking man in a houndstooth sports jacket and grey slacks, who dealt with such stuff all day and seemed untouched; who treated him as if he were a child, to be protected from the facts of life.

'Do these people know they're being photographed, Inspector?'

'Oh yes, sir. They pay for it. They take the pictures away. I only get copies because of my arrangements with the person who runs the place.'

'Can I meet her – and the girl?'

'Of course, sir. Just let me make a phone call.'

'I'd better see the films first.'

When the last reel flickered and the screen went white again Felinski knew that they were the things that would nail Yasnov. The stills could be faked, but to put another man's face on all these films would have been almost impossible.

The house just off Berkeley Square was like most of the others. Well cared for, newly painted, with window boxes and an orange tree in a tub at the door. They were shown into a small room with chintz furniture and white walls. There were bottles and glasses on the table.

The woman who came in was in her forties, surprisingly good-looking, and she held out her hand to Watkins as if he were an old friend. When Felinski had been introduced as a colleague she poured them each a drink but she didn't drink herself. She leaned forward and said, 'I understand that your friend wants to have a talk with Karen, Mr Watkins.'

'That's it. Have you been able to contact her?'

'Yes, she's here now, and I've told her that I want her to help you in any way she can.'

Watkins stood up. 'Perhaps you and I can have a few minutes together while my colleague is busy.'

The girl who came in was a cool Swedish-type blonde straight from any Hitchcock film. Nearer Grace Kelly than Kim Novak. As she sat down she reached for a cigarette from the glass on the table. She leaned back as she inhaled and Felinski said, 'Are you English, Miss Lyon?'

'If Manchester's still England, I am.'

Felinski was surprised at the quiet, attractive voice. It was hard to connect this girl with the action in the photographs. He pushed across the picture of Yasnov in the street.

'Do you recognize this man?'

'Yes, that's Boris – Boris Yasnov.'

'Are you sure that's his name?'

'Madame Yvonne checks on all clients before she does business with them. So you can take it that's his name.'

'How long has he been a client of yours?'

'Oh, about three years or maybe a bit longer.'

'How many times have you, er, operated with him?'

'Eight or nine, I'm not sure exactly.'

'Has it always been you?'

'Except once when I was abroad.'

'Why? Does he always ask for you?'

She leaned back and smiled, and he was conscious of the pretty face and the long legs. 'You're not really Vice Squad, are you?'

'No I'm not, but I still require answers.'

'If you were Vice Squad you wouldn't need to ask. Men who're real perverts want a girl who knows all their kinks. They don't want to explain each time, that turns them off. So they always want the same girl. Some of my clients have me sent over to Cairo or Athens. They pay to have me because I know what they want.'

'And what did Yasnov want?'

'Mainly masochism, some degradation.'

'How did he pay you?'

'In sterling. Once I went to him in Paris and he paid in francs.'

'Cash or cheque?'

She laughed. 'This is a cash-in-advance business, mister.'

'What did he talk about with you?'

'Sex.'

'His kind of sex or normal sex?'

'His kind of sex.'

'Was that part of the business?'

'Of course.'

'Did he say what his job was?'

'He was a diplomat.'

'Did he know about the photographs?'

'Of course, it was done openly.'

'You mean the photographer was there with you?'

'No, he was in the next room photographing through a panel. But Yasnov wanted it.'

. 'And the films?'

'Yes, he knew; he paid extra for it.'

'He took away copies?'

'Of course. They get kicks looking at it. You can't get that sort of sex in Russia or a good many other places. That's why they pay well.'

'Did anyone else see what went on, apart from the photographer?'

'I suppose the doctor knew what had gone on but he didn't actually see it.'

'What doctor?'

'For God's sake. It cuts them open, they bleed, the doctor treats them for it, puts on antibiotics.'

'Was it Yasnov's first experience of this kind of sex when he came here?'

'Yes, I'm sure of that.'

'How could you be sure?'

'There were no whip scars on him. No marks at all.'

'And now?'

'He's got scars.'

She lit another cigarette and as she blew out the smoke she looked across at him half smiling.

'He never talked about his work?'

She shook her head.

'About his family?'

She laughed. 'Only the straight sex boys do that.'

'Are all your clients like Yasnov?'

'Pretty well. I don't do straight jobs.'

'Why is that?'

'There's more money this way. I do it for money, mister.'

'What kind of man do you think Yasnov is?'

'Oh he's a tough little bastard except when he's downstairs. When it's over he's throwing his weight around again. Like the rest of them he can be charming when he wants, but it's phoney. I bet he's a gold-plated bastard in his work.'

'Miss Lyon, I'll have to ask for your passport and warn you not to leave the country until I clear you to do so.'

She shrugged. 'If Madam says so.'

'Madam *will* say so, Miss Lyon.'

When the girl left, Watkins came in and Felinski told him to go with the girl and get her passport, and to warn her about overseas trips.

He flew back to Dublin with the photographs and films, and a Queen's Messenger identity card. The material was in the Diplomatic bag for the Embassy. He was back at the hotel just before 2 a.m.

Yasnov came back from O'Malley's Farm about four in the afternoon the next day. They had given him time to get to his room and then they had gone up. They knocked and waited. As Yasnov opened the door, Voronov pushed it aside and walked in. Felinski closed it, turned the key and put it in his pocket. Yasnov walked over to the table and as he reached

126

for the telephone Voronov's big paw held his wrist like it was set in cement, and he said in Russian, 'Don't do that, comrade.'

Yasnov said angrily, 'Who are you? What do you want in here?'

Felinski too spoke in Russian. 'Sit down, Yasnov. We want to talk to you. Sit down.'

Yasnov shook his hand free from Voronov's loosening grip and moved cautiously over to one of the big armchairs.

Voronov stood behind Yasnov's chair and Felinski sat down facing him. Yasnov's brown eyes were alert and wary, and he kept his arms on the arms of the chair. His mouth was grim with anger as he spoke.

'I just want to warn you both that we are in the Republic of Ireland and I can assure you that this outrage will not go unpunished.'

Felinski held up his hand. 'Yasnov, we're here to help you. You could be in real trouble.'

Yasnov almost spat. 'What trouble? There is no trouble.'

'I mean KGB trouble.'

Yasnov closed his mouth tight and there were two blotches of anger on his cheeks. Felinski opened the tatty briefcase and pulled out a file. From the file he took out a photograph, glanced at it, and then passed it to Yasnov. He looked at it and then tore it across again and again. Felinski waited till he had finished.

'Yasnov, there are many more where that came from.'

'What is it you want?'

'Now that's more like it. Take off your jacket.'

'What the hell is this all about?'

'Just do what I say, Yasnov.'

Yasnov stood up and slid off his jacket. Voronov took it from him and placed it on a table near the wall. Yasnov stood in his good white shirt with a soft chamois leather shoulder holster under his left armpit. Voronov grinned and slid his hand round and pulled out the pistol.

'Now take off your shirt.'

Then Yasnov was naked to the waist and the scars were all too plain. Old stripes were just fine faint brown lines but they were criss-crossed with newer scars, still an angry red against the brown barrel chest. Felinski looked up at Voronov and nodded. 'Check the rest of him.'

Voronov went over Yasnov expertly and removed a cigarette lighter and the wrist-watch. The KGB had a special unit for playing games with such trinkets and he slid them into his pocket. Felinski nodded. 'Sit down, Yasnov.'

He stared at Yasnov's face for a few moments and then he said quietly, 'We want the details of the subversion operation, comrade.'

Yasnov said nothing.

Felinski waited, then when it was clear that Yasnov was not going to speak he reached sideways and sorted carefully through the briefcase. He pulled out four large brown envelopes. He placed them carefully on the table and turned to Yasnov.

'Comrade Yasnov, these four envelopes each contain the same twelve photographs of you with a Miss Karen Lyon. Two are addressed to the Soviet embassies here in Dublin and in London. The third is addressed to the Head of the KGB at the Lubyanka and the fourth to the head of the GRU. These will be posted if you do not co-operate.'

Yasnov spoke slowly but his voice trembled as he finished. 'They will not believe you. They are fakes.'

'Yasnov, the marks on your body are not fakes. And many of them are from years ago. Your colleagues will want to make a comparison with the photographs. And then there are the films and the tapes. They'll know that those were not fakes.'

Yasnov didn't move but Felinski could see the muscles stand out where he clenched his teeth and his eyes held the first signs of fear. Then he spoke, and his voice was harsh, reflecting the dry mouth that echoed the words. 'Who are you? I've seen him somewhere before.' And he jerked his head back at Voronov.

'Yasnov, we don't want to wait. Either you co-operate or we'll leave you here and post the photographs. But we'll deliver the Dublin one by hand. They'll be round here fast, Yasnov, and you'll be in the Lubyanka tomorrow. Downstairs, not upstairs.'

Yasnov looked furtively at the brown envelopes on the table and then back at Felinski. He knew that this wasn't a bluffing face. Anything this man said he would do, he would do. It was true that the bastards from the Embassy would be round in minutes after they saw the photographs, and after that they'd have no mercy. He was conscious of his own voice saying harshly, 'What exactly do you want?'

'Let's start with O'Malley's Farm.'

When Felinski said that, Yasnov knew it was no good playing games. They obviously knew a lot already.

They had talked, and Felinski had made notes, for almost three hours and they were still only halfway through the Dublin *apparat* when Felinski broke off the interrogation. Felinski looked enquiringly at Voronov who nodded, 'Yasnov, we'll take a break now. What do you want to do?'

'What do you mean? I am here, what can I do?'

'I don't mean right now. If you co-operate with us we can co-operate with you. What do you want?'

Yasnov shrugged and pursed his lips. 'You tell me, comrade. You will decide, not me.'

Felinski decided to play it slow and stupid.

'You like to work for us?'

Yasnov shook his head. 'Never. They would get me in a month.'

'What about a pension and a place to live in America?'

Yasnov looked up quickly. So they were CIA.

'You give me protection?'

'Of course.'

Yasnov looked very pleasant. 'Maybe we can talk about this more.'

Felinski smiled. 'We'd like you to come with us.'

'Where to?'

'To London. Nice and quietly.'

For the first time Yasnov looked really defeated. The adrenalin had stopped and now it was the let-down. That was why Felinski had waited.

Felinski went to the telephone and called Maxwell. 'Yes,' he said, 'Do it now.'

Half an hour later Maxwell had arrived. He gave them a spare passport and after they had gone he let in two of the SIS team and they went over the room inch by inch. They packed what they found in a carrier bag, and after almost two hours they left.

Chapter 19

The driver took them to within a couple of hundred yards of the border. The others were waiting and they were over the border ten minutes later. There was a helicopter in a field, rotors turning idly. It took them to the airport at Belfast. The RAF flew them to Northolt, and they went by car to Laker's Farm. They were expected, a fire was burning, and Mrs Weeks fried eggs and bacon. The American exchange farmer had moved out to the spare room in the Weeks's cottage.

Felinski had decided that the farm was the most secure hide-out for Yasnov while he was under interrogation. It was going to create local problems but not so many problems as Yasnov in London. An FSP sergeant stood guard in Yasnov's room and all concerned had slept until almost midday. By then the files were down from Curzon Street and Felinski's study was laid out with trestle tables. There was a Security Signals caravan in the field behind the farm-house, and the results of Yasnov's interrogation went through to the Embassy in Dublin, and on to Maxwell. He had moved into the American Embassy after the others had left.

Among the stuff that Maxwell had found in Yasnov's room was a ten-page typescript in Russian. Maxwell didn't speak or read Russian but he'd sent it over in the Diplomatic bag. They'd also found a bundle of forged British passports and a selection of KGB devices. They had removed the diode from the phone and a micro-dot reader from the bathroom.

By early evening the interrogation was going well. They'd go over it again as they checked the information on the ground, and there was a mass of detail to be sifted and evaluated.

Felinski phoned the girl at eight that evening.
'Lavender?'
'Steve, you're back. Are you at the farm?'
'Yes. Can I come over?'
'Of course, shall I come and pick you up in the MG?'

'Fine, I'll start walking. I'll be on the short lane.'

'Are you all right, Steve?'

'Of course. Why?'

'You sound kind of funny. Tense or something. You haven't changed your mind have you?'

'Not an inch, honey. What about you?'

'Don't be silly. Well, I'll get the car out. Bye.'

They met just over a mile from the farm. As he got to the top of the small hill he could see the headlights twisting and turning as she followed the road across the marsh. He stood against the big elm and waited for her. She saw him at the last minute, and the small white car squealed to a stop and she flung herself out.

It was nearly an hour later, after he'd heard all the gossip of the Romney Marshes, that she asked about the farm. 'Steve, what's going on at the farm? Daddy said he saw a caravan at the back by the stables, and there's an army jeep and lots of coming and going.'

'It's part of what took me away, honey.'

'You nearly said "Don't worry your pretty little head". Steve.'

He laughed. 'I didn't nearly say that. Look sweetie, it's something to do with what I did in the war and I can't talk about it yet.'

They had had coffee back at the rectory, and then she'd driven him back to the bend in the lane where it led to the farm. He'd watched her turn, and had seen the car's lights thrown up to the trees as she drove up the hill.

It was late on the day after Yasnov had left the hotel that the two KGB men from the Embassy had gone over his room. They knew in five minutes that he'd flown. The empty talcum tin in the bathroom that had housed the micro-dot reader, and the missing diode on the telephone, only underlined the basic fact.

It was an hour later when others started going through his desk at the Lubyanka. Another team were examining his apartment. There was nothing suspicious, nothing out of order, at either place. But on checking his desk they distributed his files of work in process to two of his juniors. It was one of those who read Yasnov's notes on Leggat's diary and realized their importance. They set up a team to act on the diary information

131

immediately. There was a general call to all embassies to take urgent steps to trace Yasnov. A three-man team was flown to Dublin to trace Yasnov's movements and contacts. And Ulyanenko at the Soviet Embassy in London got a personal call from Semichastny to put a team on to tracing Felinski and Voronov and taking suitable action.

It was Voronov who had first rumbled Yasnov. They were sitting in Felinski's study, having a break from the interrogation. Voronov was listening to 'Raindrops are falling on my head' for the hundredth time, and sipping a glass of milk. He was beginning to fancy himself as a swinger. Felinski was reading *Farmers' Weekly* and groaning as he read out the packing station prices for eggs. When the music finished Voronov was sorting through the singles when he said, 'Jesus, we must be getting old, Steve: that bugger's taking us for a ride.'

Felinski turned on the leather stool. 'I'd bet my life on what we've got out of him.'

Voronov shook his head and waved the hand with the empty glass. 'Look Steve, Yasnov and I went through the same training. He wants to do a deal, yes. So he's going to keep something in hand. That's what I'd do and that's what he's doing.'

'So?'

'So we go through the motions of the deal. We'll do it together. You'll have to talk about the deal because he won't believe that I could do a deal. And he's right. I'll chip in and give him the jump when you've almost settled. Do it carefully, don't throw the pennies around or he'll know it's phoney. Make him graft for it.'

An hour later Felinski was talking to Franks. 'We've got something important out of Yasnov that your political friends should know. The Special Collection has been put into neutral by the Presidium. They've OK'd the continuing subversion in the UK but the Special Collection isn't an operation now. It's been put back to planning only.'

'Well that's good news. The Americans will like that. You're satisfied he's not bluffing?'

'He's not bluffing because the rest of his story is that the KGB and the Army are going it alone. They won't call off the Special Collection.'

There was a long silence at the other end and then Franks said, 'What are you going to do?'

'I've kicked it around with Voronov and we both think that breaking up the subversion networks is number one priority. Without that going successfully the boys are going to think again. And if we are in any doubt, somebody at the FO can slip the word to Brezhnev. Be better if we don't have to do that because it could make a pretty loud bang. So when we move on the arrests keep the publicity down as much as you can. Let me know if anyone disagrees with our basic evaluation.'

'Fine. Shall I pass the news to Maxwell?'

'Yes, you do that. His people should be pleased. It looks like the balance they were after is as important in Moscow as it is in Washington. Just the wild boys causing trouble.'

There was a report from SIS Dublin that another KGB man appeared to be liaising with the group, but there were no more meetings. The group had obviously been ordered to lie low until things had been sorted out.

Voronov had translated the pages of typescript that had come over from the search of Yasnov's room. It covered the whole of the Dublin network into the UK and it gave enough names and details for most of them to be identified and picked up. But it wasn't time for that yet. Felinski radioed the details for Special Branch surveillance to Curzon Street.

There were only two lights shining on the ninth floor of one of the high-rise office blocks near Victoria Station. And there was only one man in the two offices. The air-conditioning made a low humming noise that seemed to vibrate the air in the big office. The man was young and as he sat at the computer terminal he looked tense and nervous. He was looking at the digital clock mounted on the far wall. This was only the second criminal act that he had ever done. The first was not very serious, he'd allowed a friend to borrow his passport. When it came back ten days later he wasn't sure whether he was pleased or frightened when he saw the French immigration stamps inside. He hadn't thought about it too long and there had never been any repercussions.

There was, in fact, one repercussion, but he wasn't aware of it. One of the duties of local Communist Party branches is to recruit for the KGB people who could be useful to them. Generally there was a member in each branch responsible for selecting possible recruits and it always followed the same ritual. The potential recruit was asked to do some small deed that was demonstrably illegal, something for the Party. If they did it without demur they were on the slippery path. They'd done something that could be used as a pressure point and it meant that if they would do something mildly illegal once, they would do something obviously illegal next time. Some were flattered at the trust displayed in them but some were a little frightened at the same time. Harold Marks had been a computer operator and now he was a programmer and he looked down at the ten inches of print-out paper and studied it for the last time. It wasn't a program that *he* had written, but he knew what it was. They hadn't made any bones about it. As he looked at the clock it clicked up 22.45 and he pressed the release key on the terminal keyboard. He tapped out a seventeen-digit code and then as the lights flickered he typed in his request.

There had been long debates in the House, and days of debates in sub-committees, about computer security. The necessity for not allowing the police to have access to information gathered by one government department and another. Tax returns, health records and a host of other accumulated data could be useful to many police departments. Commercial data banks could help a lot too. A quick look at the big five banks' computerized data could pass many a happy hour for the Fraud Squad. But the British enjoy their game of cops and robbers and they don't like the police to have too much of a chance of catching crooks. It had to be sporting. But if you want the address of every man, woman and child with the same surname there's only one easy way to find out. It may take up to ten minutes to print-out the initials and addresses of all the Joneses or the Smiths. The police have no access to it. It's all coded and on magnetic tape in the Ministry of Health's computer centre in Gateshead. And there's a special top secret code to apply before you can even gain access to the computer.

It was that code with the seventeen digits that Harold Marks had tapped on the terminal keyboard. It seemed that there were only nine people in the UK with the particular name that he fed in, and their addresses were typed up on the fast printer in 3·4 seconds. Marks ripped off the print-out paper, folded it neatly, and stuffed it up his shirt front. He destroyed the other paper in the shredder, switched off the terminal, the printer, and the lights, and closed the door to the corridor behind him.

The Securicor man at the main entrance swopped the *Evening Standard* for Marks's *Evening News* and let him out of the building.

The print-out sheet was quite short because there were only three addresses in the whole UK where men named Felinski lived.

Chapter 20

They call them 'higglers' in Kent. Men who travel round the Romney Marsh farms buying surplus eggs, and hens at the end of their lay. The battered hand-painted green van had been parked at the farm gate and the thin man in the old army great-coat had trudged up to the inner gate and pressed the bell. It was a few minutes before anyone came, and the thin man's gaze took in the caravan with the thirty-foot whip aerials, and the army jeep and motorcycle parked in the yard by the silo.

The man who came out of one of the laying houses walked over and asked him what he wanted. It seemed there were no eggs for sale and no hens either. And all that had been said in a good Texas drawl. Just to make sure, the higgler put one last question.

'Where's the gaffer?'

'The what?'

'The gaffer, the boss, the chap I generally see.'

'I'm afraid he's busy.'

'He know they've got fowl pest over at Dymchurch?'

'No, we hadn't heard that. Is it bad?'

'I don't rightly know guv'nor, but you ought to tell him.'

'I'll do that. Thanks for letting me know.'

The higgler turned as if to go, then swung back, hesitating. 'Give Mr Felinski my regards, will you.'

'I'll certainly do that. Good morning to you.'

The 'higgler' hadn't looked back but he had seemed to have trouble starting the van. He got it started but it stalled in the lane in front of the farm-house. A Field Security sergeant came down the path, but the van started jerkily before he got to the small gate in the low hedge. But he was near enough for the 'higgler' to see the green Intelligence Corps flashes.

The 'higgler' had only been tolerated in the pub at Appledore, but over his pint he'd learned a lot about the man who farmed down the road to Rye.

His companion in the back of the green van had laid low like Brer Rabbit and said nothing. But it was he who gave the report to the man from the Soviet Embassy when they met later that day at the Golden Egg in Leicester Square.

The other two surveillance teams had drawn blanks but there wasn't much doubt where their quarry lay. And apart from anything else they'd seen Voronov at one of the windows.

Felinski had been surprised at the strength of the KGB networks in Glasgow and London, and he and Voronov had interrogated Yasnov to a point near exhaustion. Felinski himself felt near the end of his tether. Names and addresses, code-words and dead-drops swirled through his head, and he finally called Maxwell to come back and take over the analysis of the networks before they went in to pick them up. SIS never picked up a whole network, they always left a couple of middle-graders on the loose. If you didn't do that you were working blind on the next network the Soviets set up. If you leave a couple free then you can watch the new network being built up around them, and you know where you are. It's risky, but a complete clear-out has you right in the dark again.

Maxwell had spent the next day planning the round-up of the Glasgow, Midlands and London networks. The resources of Special Branch were now seriously over-extended and Maxwell had asked for CIA help. And help from CID, for the two days before the arrests, and for the arrests themselves.

Voronov and Felinski had kept up the pressure on Yasnov and a security clerk was typing pages of signed statements.

It was just before eight that evening that Felinski decided he'd had enough, and he phoned the girl.

'Lavender?'

'No it's not Lavender, Steve. It's her mother.'

'Is Lavender around, mother? I thought I'd come over.'

'But she's with you, dear.'

And right then, as if all his training and all his experience had been funnelled into one single micro-second, Felinski knew. But he went on. He needed the details.

'Tell me what happened.'

'Nothing happened, dear. She went off straight away as soon as your friend came over.'

'When was this?'

'Oh dear me, about an hour and a half or maybe two hours.' Then the first surge of doubt and worry. 'You mean she hasn't seen you, Steve?'

'No. I'm afraid she hasn't. Now listen carefully. If the phone rings don't answer it. I'm coming over at once. I'll be there in fifteen minutes.'

He was there in ten.

'What was the man like?'

The tears were very near and her voice trembled.

'A young man, Steve. Spoke nicely. A smiling sort of boy. Tall and quite good-looking. A sports coat and slacks.'

'What did he say?'

'He said you'd sent him for Lavender. That you were going into Rye and she could go with you.' She looked at him and her voice broke. 'She was so pleased Steve, and we never thought . . .' and then the tears took over. There was no point in asking anything else. They'd have changed cars inside ten minutes. He'd lose time getting back to the farm but it would be better to say nothing more in front of the distraught woman. He fetched Lavender's father from the church and told him he would phone later.

Felinski phoned the news of the girl's kidnapping to Curzon Street, and waited for the inevitable phone call. As he paced up and down he heard the voices of Voronov and Yasnov in the next room. It was midnight when the phone rang, and Felinski forced himself to wait for six rings before he picked up the earpiece. The voice was public school and very cool.

'Mr Felinski?'

'Speaking.'

'I think we've both lost something, Mr Felinski, do you fancy making an exchange?'

'What are you talking about?'

'Oh dear, Mr Felinski, don't let us play games.'

'What have you got in mind?'

'Nothing complicated, Mr Felinski, a straight exchange.'

'When?'

'That's up to you. You can choose the time, we choose the place.'

'Where have you got in mind?'

'Let's say one of the embassies.'

'Which one?'

The speaker laughed softly. 'We'll let you know.'

'When?'

'I said we'll leave that to you.'

'Two o'clock tomorrow, today that is.'

The phone clicked, the caller had hung up. Felinski played the tape back to Curzon Street.

Voronov's eyes were bloodshot with fatigue, but he spoke as if the day had just started.

'There's not much more to get, Steve.'

Felinski looked at him. 'What are you thinking of?'

'Why not trade him for the girl? That's what they want.'

Felinski shook his head. 'He's a prime witness. He could testify in court.'

'You're going to have a hundred or so who can be put on trial. It's just a matter of time now till all the networks are in the bag. What do we need Yasnov for?'

'Most of the networks are our nationals. A colonel in the KGB who gives evidence of the operation is a real clincher.'

'No he's not, Steve. You know better than that. The Russians will say he's insane, or that it's a put-up job – all the usual stuff.'

'Why do they want him back then?'

'The main reason is to have a scapegoat when you do the big exposure. He's going to be the big bad wolf who planned it all in secret. Helped by British and United States Intelligence, of course. He gets them all off the hook. That's why they want him, comrade.'

Felinski didn't reply. He was sitting looking out of the big farm window. Voronov waited a few minutes and then spoke again.

'What do your people want to do about the girl and Yasnov?'

'They left it up to me.'

Voronov walked over to the side table and poured himself a whisky.

'You want a drink, Steve?'

'Not right now.'

There was a long silence and then Voronov put down his empty glass. 'Why did you tell them to phone at two o'clock?'

'God knows. I just wanted time to think.'

'You realize that they won't make the exchange then?'

Felinski turned quickly. 'Why not?'

'They're trying you out. Checking if you would, or could, make a deal. They'll come back with more demands. The longer they hold you off, keep you on the end of a phone, the more time they've got to warn their networks. Let's not kid ourselves, a lot of important heads are rolling right now in the Moscow Centre and there'll be more to come. People will be looking for scapegoats and the likely ones will be working like dogs to keep out of trouble.'

Voronov looked up sympathetically at Felinski's drawn face. He was moving from anxiety to fear, and it was beginning to show. Voronov was sure that the Russians wouldn't do a straight exchange, they were just trying Felinski for size. It looked to Voronov as though Leggat had talked before he died. He was the only man inside the Moscow Centre who would have heard of Felinski. But even as he was thinking he realized that they would have automatically put Felinski's name on the computer to see if there were any other leads or traces and the name would have come up in Voronov's own post-war interrogation. That was years back but the cards and names and details had all been put on the Central Records data bank. It wouldn't help them much, but it would back up Leggat's story. And they'd know that Yasnov would have been sucked dry by now. The girl was going to be just the opening gambit.

Yasnov was asleep. Exhausted and trembling, he had sat there, no longer capable of absorbing their questions. The doctor had given him a shot and there would be an eight-hour gap in the interrogation. There was very little left that he had to give them.

They were playing over the tapes covering the last two Special Collection meetings, and his briefing from Semichastny. Felinski pressed the stop button and looked across at Voronov. Voronov was half smiling.

'Why the smile, Kliment?'

'I was just thinking the same as you were thinking.'

'You mean Moscow?'

Voronov nodded but he didn't speak. But his eyes were sharp on Felinski's face.

'Have we got his number?'

'Semichastny's? Yes, it's in the first few pages of the transcript.'

'What if he isn't there?'

'He'll be there. He'll sleep there till this is over.'

'What will the general reaction be in Moscow at the moment?'

'The Presidium will wonder what the hell is going on, because they only know half the story. They'll think the British are over-reacting to a couple of KGB networks – and they'll probably be wondering why the KGB are over-reacting too.'

'And the KGB?'

'No doubt about them. They'll be desperate to get back to square one. But they won't be able to sell that idea to Rudovsky and Voroshilov. Not without a bloody good reason.'

'And we could give them the reason.'

'Yes. But it's got to look like a deal. If you make it a threat and they've got to back down, then they'll be looking for a chance to raise hell somewhere else just to show they're still in business.'

'But if we let them off the hook they can try it on again.'

Voronov shook his head. 'First, you don't let them off the hook. You throw out a hundred or so of the Embassy Staff. You put on trial your own nationals and any others you collect from the networks. And you give them back Yasnov. They'll want a scapegoat to put on trial, and Yasnov fills the bill.'

'And the girl?'

Voronov shook his head. 'Don't even mention her. That would leave you wide open to all sorts of dilution.'

Felinski phoned Franks and outlined the scheme so that he could get Foreign Office agreement. In the end it was the Prime Minister who gave the Cabinet's clearance. Special telephone operators were in place an hour later at Tunbridge Wells and London. Felinski heard the London operator checking that it was Semichastny himself at the other end. Finally the London Security Signals operator referred to Yasnov and Semichastny

141

acknowledged quickly that he was on the line. The special line was clear of static and Felinski could sense the tension at the other end as the cold voice interjected with several questions. When Felinski had laid down his conditions there had been a short silence at the other end, and then Semichastny had asked if any Soviet diplomat had been informed. Satisfied that this was not the case, he asked for the return of Yasnov. Felinski agreed. He then asked for an undertaking that the Press would not be told, and that when the Embassy staff were declared *personae non gratae* the networks would be the only reason given. Even when assured on this he pressed the point that the Party and the Ministry of Foreign Affairs would react very strongly because they would not know the basic reason. Felinski confirmed that that was expected and would be handled carefully. Finally Semichastny overreached and asked for Voronov to be returned. Felinski refused, and countered by asking Semichastny for some indication of his ability to call off the Special Collection total operation. There were a few moments' silence and then Semichastny said he knew of no way to establish this. Felinski waited for a few seconds to let the point go home, and then he asked for a photostat copy of the minutes of the last meeting of the Special Collection to be passed to the British Embassy in Moscow. Semichastny hesitated, then offered its delivery to the British Embassy in Paris. Felinski accepted, and then asked for a copy of the next meeting's minutes. Semichastny swore crudely and after a short silence, agreed. Felinski had checked over the details once again and that had been it. There were no pleasantries, not a second's relaxation, and that satisfied Felinski. So far as Semichastny could control the situation, everyone was back to square one. The balance would exist once again.

When two o'clock passed and there had been no further contact about the girl, Felinski realized that for almost a day he had been neutralized. He phoned Franks, who drove down immediately.

'Steve, I know how unhappy you must be about this. Do you want to pull out?'

'No. There's so much in my mind, this whole business is a mass of detail . . .'

The phone rang and Felinski grabbed for it, dropped it and retrieved it.

'Yes, who is it?'

'Evening, Felinski, afraid I've got bad news for you.'

Felinski said nothing, he dreaded what they might say but he had enough control to wait. Then the voice went on. 'Here's somebody else to have a word with you,' and almost without a break Felinski heard a hard, grating voice speaking in Russian. 'We want you to stop any action against our people, Felinski, otherwise we kill the girl.' And the phone went dead.

Almost three minutes later the phone rang again. It was Security Signals for Franks. He listened and finally said quietly, 'Yes, leave it to me.' He turned to Felinski.

'Steve, we've traced the call.'

'But they dialled, they didn't come through the operator.'

'True, but we've put a special team on five main junctions. We could have covered the wrong ones but as it happens we were lucky.'

'Where were they?'

'A block of flats in Putney. We'd got the flat located before they hung up. There's an SIS team on its way to take over. Do you want to go yourself?'

Felinski nodded. The numbness was melting away. 'Will you take care of Lavender's parents? The police are there already, I mean try and keep them calm.'

'Get on your way, Steve. Use my car. I'll cover for you here with Voronov and Maxwell till you get back.'

Franks went into the study and beckoned to Voronov. Yasnov was asleep in an armchair and the Field Security sergeant was sitting facing him. Franks closed the door quietly and led Voronov into the sitting-room.

'Sit down.'

He told Voronov what had happened.

'How much more do you need from Yasnov?'

Voronov looked up alertly. He sensed what was coming. 'Nothing. There are details we could get. A few names he can't yet recall, but we've got all we need.'

'Right. I want you to deal with Yasnov.'

Voronov's eyes were on Franks's face and he looked at him

without blinking for a few moments before he spoke. 'You realize they'll kill the girl.'

'Steve will get there in two hours, so she'll be safe enough.'

Voronov stood up slowly and walked across to the side-table where the drinks were laid out. He poured himself a vodka and then turned and leaned against the wall. As he took a good half of the drink he let it run down to his stomach and then looked over at Franks. They'd never learn. They were so much better than the KGB. The KGB weren't in the same league. But they'd never really understand the Soviet way. They evaluated on their own standards. They couldn't grasp the cunning peasant mind, the brutality, the indifference to life. He tossed back the rest of the vodka, closed his eyes for a moment, and then without looking back at Franks he said, 'The girl won't be there. She'll be out of the country by now. At best she'll be on a boat at one of the ports, but even that's unlikely.'

'What makes you think that?'

Voronov sighed and folded his arms. 'I was one of them, Mr Franks.'

'They wouldn't take her out of the country just to kill her.'

'Look, they've got a pressure point on Felinski. They've merely protected their weapon. If they don't get what they want they'd kill her. And they'll want a lot more than Yasnov.'

'So Yasnov isn't important?'

'That's not so. They'll want somebody to take the blame. If you just close down their networks they'll say you're crushing the workers, but if Yasnov is put on trial in London they know that half the world will believe you people. If he goes back to Moscow they've got someone they can blame, a show trial, or such-like, then they will take away a lot of your credibility.'

Franks looked across at Voronov and said quietly, 'I'm sure you're right, Kliment. Nevertheless, Yasnov must not be available – ever.'

'And the girl?'

'I'm afraid I can't take that into consideration.'

'And Felinski?'

Franks didn't dodge the two cold grey eyes or the grim mouth. 'He needn't know for some time. I'll say we've removed Yasnov now that he's finished talking, so that we can make arrangements for his return.'

'And when he does know. When he knows that what he arranged with Semichastny was ignored. And because of that the girl is dead. Then what?'

'It will break him up. It will be terrible.'

It had been Voronov who gave the coffee to Yasnov but Franks had stood and watched. As Yasnov tasted the bitter flavour he had pulled a face and looked up at the big Russian. Then his eyes closed tight and a gentle sigh came from him. A few seconds later it was Franks who felt the inert pulse. An ambulance came just before dawn and a little later headed back towards London.

Voronov had slept through to midday. There was no news from Felinski. While he shaved, Voronov had tried to push out of his mind the thought of Felinski's grief when he learned about the girl. Maybe he'd never definitely know. But Voronov knew instinctively that Moscow Centre would recognize the damage they could do by letting the Englishman know that they had squared the account for not returning Yasnov, and that there was nothing to come back to any more. When he had finished shaving, he dressed, and as he put on his heavy coat he knew that he could never be the one who told Felinski. The one who waited while the news sank home.

As he walked down the lane he almost passed the red kiosk. As the door closed behind him he started reading the instructions in the telephone directory. He had talked for twenty minutes and they'd said it would take three days. They'd brushed aside his first proposition but they bought the second.

Chapter 21

The block of flats was what estate agents and developers call luxury apartments, but outwardly they had all the functional severity of a pre-war hospital. Red facing-bricks, metal window frames and large double doors that led into a small carpeted foyer. There were three blocks. One long one, with four entrance lobbies, and two shorter blocks that enclosed the well-tended garden area. The gardens sloped down from a glass kiosk housing a porter, to the long block. Felinski had parked the car in the visitors' parking space, and a plainclothes CID man had walked over to him as he looked across at Putney Heath. There was an administration office near a block of garages and that was where the SIS controller was waiting. He was a smallish, red-headed Scot, and he was bent over a table as they went in, looking at a map and an architectural plan. He looked up as the door opened and then smiled. 'Glad to see you, sir. It's all under control.'

'How many are there?'

'Only two. We've identified one of them. He's one of the boys from the second network, came over here after the Hungarian trouble in 'fifty-six. Works on the international telephone exchange. Name of Gabor. The other one's much younger. They've made a couple of telephone calls. We've got tapes and transcripts. Gabor called the home of a member of the Soviet Embassy. Didn't say much but they were leaning on him from the other end to get a move on. The young fellow spoke to his girlfriend. We've checked on her. Could be complications there, sir. She's staying at the Irish Embassy, very pretty girl, a senator's daughter, Irish senator that is. She's on your central identities list, Sara Mathews.'

'Miss Coombs is not in the flat then?'

The little Scot looked serious as he spoke quietly. 'I'm afraid not, sir.'

'You'd better show me the layout.'

'Right, sir. They're in this flat in the long block. You go in

146

Entrance Two, and it's on the ground floor on the righthand side. We've got a key but it could be bolted on the other side. When you get inside there's a longish hallway. Three main rooms on the right, kitchen, bathroom, toilet, and two more rooms on the left. We're watching the front and back, two men apiece, and I've got one of my men on the stairs a couple of flights up.'

'Have you got small arms?'

'Sure. A Smith and Wesson three eight or a Luger. Which d'you prefer?'

'I'll have the Luger.'

Felinski had given the SIS man five minutes to warn his men and then he had strolled down the path that edged the lawns. All the windows of the flat looking on to the gardens were closed with Venetian blinds, but light shone through the slats from the main-room windows. He pushed through the big swing doors and stood in the foyer.

From the flat on the left he could hear the signature tune of ITN's 'News at Ten'. The door on the right was solid oak. He bent down and laid the jemmy quietly on the tiled floor. There was vaseline on the key and it slid silently into the lock. There was no resistance as it turned, and he pushed gently and slowly on the door. It was not bolted, and he opened it only enough to look in. The far end of the hallway was in shadow but the end near the door was well lit. There was a large plant in a stone jar on the lefthand side and there was a light on in the kitchen on the left. He eased himself in slowly. Away from the sounds of the foyer he could hear voices, and a radio was playing jazz. He quietly closed the door and stood still. Somebody laughed in the room. They were both in there. He put his hand in his pocket and pushed down the safety catch. He eased the pistol out and held the silencer with his left hand as he found a good grip with his right. He would have to take two steps to reach the door, and with the first they might see his shadow in the square, frosted-glass panels that gave light from the room to the hall. He took the first step, reached for the bronze handle, and gently opened the door.

They were both sitting, and the fair-haired youth was laughing. The laugh froze and he made to get up.

'Keep still both of you.'

The other man, Gabor, stubbed out his cigarette and looked back at Felinski. Nobody asked what he was doing there but they had both noticed that the Luger didn't waver. He looked at the youth.

'Where's the girl?'

The youth smirked and touched his hair where it fell in a wave to his cheek. 'What girl?' he said.

The silencer had hissed sharply, and between the boy's suède shoes there were two large splinters of white wood from the floor, and a gash in the green carpet. The other man shifted uncomfortably.

'The next time I'll aim higher and the senator's daughter won't like that.' He jerked the pistol angrily at the youth who looked paralysed with fear.

'She's not here.' His mouth was open as fear tightened his throat. Then he screamed as the pistol lined up on his groin. He held up his hand as if to ward off the slug. 'Don't, don't, I'll tell you.' Felinski kept the gun aimed at him and the boy was swaying backwards and forwards in agitation. 'Oh my God, they'll kill me. They'll kill me.' It was then that the Hungarian had launched himself. The slug had stopped him halfway as it hammered his knee-cap into fragments, and he fell back into the chair with his head jerking in pain. His hand went to touch his knee, but the pain was too great, and as his hand clenched, he fainted.

The youth was trembling and his eyes were on Felinski's face. 'Please don't do it. I'll tell you where she is.'

'Where?'

'She's in the Republic.'

'Where?'

'At a farm.'

'O'Malley's Farm?'

The youth's mouth opened. 'You know then.'

'Was it you who picked her up from Tenterden?'

'Yes.'

'Who gave you your orders? Who told you what to do?'

The youth pointed at his unconscious companion. 'He told me what to do. The man from the Soviet Embassy took over later.'

'Which man from the Embassy? What's his name?'

'Something like Yulansky. I can't remember.'

'How did they take her?'

'A private plane from a place in Yorkshire. A man named Uncle Tom owns it. I don't know his real name. There's a small landing strip at the farm, for crop-spraying planes.'

'What else do you do for them?'

'Just take messages, and I've helped them on jobs.'

'What jobs?'

'When people get out of line.'

'How much do they pay you?'

'They don't.'

'What do you get?'

The boy looked pale and there was a pulse beating in his neck. 'I do it for Sara.'

'She's your girl?'

The boy shook his head. 'No, she's the Dutchman's girl.'

'What do you get out of it then?'

'She lets me sleep with her when I do jobs.'

'What's your name?'

'Peter Curtis.'

Felinski stared at him. 'Are you Sir Peter's son?'

The boy nodded.

Sir Peter Curtis was the chief executive of one of the nationalized industries.

Felinski had left the SIS team to clear up the mess, but had warned them not to charge the youth, or the newspapers would start following up the story.

Felinski drove on to Curzon Street and phoned Franks and Maxwell. He checked the files on the Soviet Embassy staff and picked out Ulyanenko. He had not told Franks what he planned to do about the girl, but Franks was too shrewd a man not to have guessed. The ring-leaders of the networks were to be arrested and charged, in an operation that would start in forty-eight hours. Maxwell had organized the operation with Special Branch and they had brought in the CID in major towns. Word seemed to have gone to the various groups in the subversive networks to go carefully. Activities had been much reduced.

Felinski knew that there was no chance of leaving the recovery of the girl to the Irish authorities. They never hurried for the

English, whatever was at stake. By the time it had been discussed and authenticated to some Minister's satisfaction it would be too late. The girl would be dead. Felinski sensed that the control of the main operation was slipping away from him but it was mainly routine now. And he needed to act swiftly. When the arrests began, the girl's fate would be sealed. He had sat with Tim MacNay for an hour, and then MacNay had made a dozen phone calls. When he had finished he looked elated. 'Steve, I've got a crew and a boat. They're all the best. If you do your stuff they'll be ready when you get there.'

The Irish Embassy in London is not renowned for its architectural beauty. It's a rather dirty, gloomy pile on the corner of Grosvenor Place and Chester Street. Taxis turn there to get to smarter places. At night it looks even gloomier and there are seldom any lights visible inside. It always has a police constable on guard. He is not there, despite the troubles, to guard its occupants from the English, but rather to guard them from some faction or other of their own countrymen who don't like what is being done, or not done, in their name.

Felinski had phoned the girl from a box in Belgrave Square. She had been suspicious at first when he said he was calling on behalf of the boy, but when he mentioned Ulyanenko she said she'd meet him on the corner in five minutes. Then he saw her. Coming down the steps in Chester Street she had on some light colour, and as she crossed the road he saw that she was even prettier than the photographs in her dossier. She followed him up Grosvenor Place and he turned into Halkin Street and stopped.

'Miss Mathews?'

She looked up at him and the big green eyes studied his face. 'Has something gone wrong?'

'I'll leave it to Ulyanenko to tell you. I'm just sent to fetch you.'

'We'll have to hurry. I can't stay long. Where is Uly?'

He smiled. 'Let's go, shall we?'

He opened the car door for her and then got in the other side. He nodded to the driver and they headed west. The girl lit a cigarette and gazed out of the windows. It wasn't until she

150

recognized Shepherd's Bush that she spoke. 'My God, we're at Shepherd's Bush. Where the hell are we going?'

'We're going to Dublin, Miss Mathews, to the farm.'

She turned to look at him. 'Who in hell are you? You're not from Uly or Peter,' and she reached for the door handle. Felinski's hand wrapped round her wrist. 'Don't try anything silly, Miss Mathews, or you'll get hurt.'

She leaned back and he knew she was trying to work out what she should do. There was an RAF guard on the gates when they arrived at Northolt and he knew she must have seen the big wooden board with the name of the airfield.

He'd left the girl at the guardroom. She had a more appreciative audience there. The adjutant had a message from Tim MacNay. The team had already gone and would be waiting for him at Ardglass. The aircrew were ready for their flight to Belfast. The girl stopped talking when he went into the guardroom and the pretty face lost its animation.

They sat buckled in the twin seats, and as the jet thundered to take-off the girl put her hand on Felinski's arm and closed her eyes. The plane clawed its steep flight up through the clouds and at four thousand feet they were above the cloud level, and the moonlight shone on the cumulus ocean beneath them. The shadow of the plane leaped and plunged ahead and below. Then the cloud broke and way below them they could see the sparkle on the sea. The girl had kept her hand resting on his arm, and after looking down at the sea she turned and looked at him as she spoke.

'They'll kill the girl if you make any attempt on the farm.'

Felinski looked at her and said, 'Then it would be your turn, Miss Mathews.'

'Mother of God. You call me "Miss" when you tell me you'll murder me.'

'Do you go to Mass?'

'From time to time.'

'Then pray that your friends don't harm the girl.'

'Don't you people realize that we're not on our own this time? England's finished, it's just a question of days. What you're doing now is pointless. If you kill me it won't make any difference.'

'And the Republic? What will the Russians do there?'

Her eyes blazed and he knew he'd touched a sore spot. 'We'll make some changes sure, but by God we'll have taught you bastards a lesson first. You'll be building *our* bloody roads for a change.'

'And the Americans?'

'And what would this whole thing be to them?'

Felinski waited. 'So your friends haven't told you what it's really about.' He paused and then went on.

'The Russians will follow this up with a nuclear attack on the United States.'

The anger was there again. 'You lying bastard. This is your turn, not the Americans'.'

They were coming down fast and they could see the airport lights coming up to meet them. It wasn't an airliner landing and they were dropping fast. They bounced on the runway and then the plane shuddered in the deafening noise of the jets reversing. They taxied to a small bay with a hangar, and men in RAF uniforms put up a metal ladder for them. It was freezing cold on the tarmac and the girl shivered.

The car got them to Ardglass in an hour. They went straight to the quay. Alongside a wooden pontoon was an air-sea rescue launch. The kind that can slice through the sea at 35 knots. All the RAF roundels had been painted out and a man in a bosun's chair was painting out the number on her prow. The lights from the saloon flooded on to the jetty and the sound of voices carried across the water. Tim MacNay helped them both into the cockpit.

'Is there a cabin for the girl, Tim?'

'Aye, but we'll give her a guard all the same – we don't want any damage done, do we?'

When they were alone, MacNay poured him a whisky into a plastic mug.

'There's trouble back in London, Steve. Voronov's gone missing. They're throwing fits. He went missing lunchtime yesterday. Didn't take any kit with him – nothing. Seems he phoned Curzon Street late yesterday evening. Said he'd got a message for you. Here – I've got it written down somewhere.' He fished in his anorak pocket and pulled out a folded card. As he handed it over he said, 'Voronov said he would dictate the message because it must be exact.'

Felinski unfolded the card and moved to one of the bulkhead lights. The card read, 'The bridge is wrecked stop They will not kill the girl stop Kliment Ivanovich Voronov stop.'

MacNay waved his drink. 'I read it Steve, in case it was operational. Couldn't make head nor tail of it. What do you make of it?'

Felinski was silent for a few moments. He wasn't exactly sure what it meant. The meaning was just on the edge of his mind. Like coming out of a dream, aware of the dream but not of its content. He slid it into his pocket. 'Not quite sure, Tim, not quite sure.'

Chapter 22

Tim MacNay called to Felinski, 'Steve, come and meet the skipper.'

The man who held his hand out was over six foot with a beard to match. But the beard was neater than his clothes. He wore an oil-stained battle-dress jacket and a pair of trousers that looked like the remnants of a track-suit. On his feet were tatty suède shoes but the tanned face was cheerful and alert.

MacNay said, 'This is Commander Andrews, Steve, RN.'

Andrews's hand was big and his grip was confident. 'Hello, Steve. I'd better make very clear that I'm RN on leave. The Admiralty Board wouldn't approve of this little lark at all. I was working it out on the way over with Tim, it came to twenty-three offences, and if I can think of twenty-three, those chaps could think of more. All the Navy boys are on leave. They've got proper passes because I issued them myself. There's two paratroopers, but Tim looked after them.'

Andrews went down the companionway into the main saloon and Felinski and MacNay followed him. There were five men sitting on the foam bunks, and on the sole-boards were newspapers covered with bits and pieces of sub-machine guns. Andrews nodded as they looked up. 'OK chaps, this is Steve and he's in charge.' He turned to Felinski. 'Let me introduce them. Going round the circle there's Paul with the beautiful curls, the ugly one is Ted, then there's Frank and Leslie, they're two of my boys, and this is Peter. Tom's looking after the girl and where's Joe?'

'In the heads.'

'Well, that's the motley crew.'

Felinski leaned against the bulkhead and looked around the group. 'I'd better explain that what we're going to do is completely unauthorized. If we make a bog of it there'll be a hell of a row. What we are going to do would raise a storm if we did it in England. To do it in the Republic could cause real trouble. I say this merely to show that we can't take any risks. We've got

154

to be successful and we've got to be quick. And if possible nobody gets hurt. Us or them.' Felinski turned to MacNay. 'Have you got the aerial photographs, Tim, and the maps?'

The maps and the photographs were laid on the saloon table. Felinski described the farm, its buildings and the approaches and finally covered the two routes from the harbour. Almost at the end of his talk Andrews put his head inside the saloon. 'Can you spare a minute, Steve?'

In the cockpit, Andrews was leaning over a chart-table, and his dividers were stalking over two charts and laying off distances on a scale. As he worked he spoke without looking up.

'The trip is near as damn it sixty miles. With normal crew I could do it in two to three hours. But we've got a lot of extra weight and a Force four. Doesn't sound much but this is a planing boat and if I goose her too hard it'll be like riding into a brick wall. I'm going to take four to four and a half hours. That means we'll have about two hours to carry out your little plan. There'll probably be almost an hour's darkness after that, but if we stay that long I'll lose the tide, and the inner section of the harbour dries out anyway. I don't want to be stranded.'

'That should be enough time for us. It's not a finely timed plan, it's a bit rough and ready.'

'That's OK as long as we all know what we're at.' Andrews called up to a man on the jetty. 'Sailor, leave one turn round the bollard and lead it to me.' The man stooped and uncoiled the rope and led the bitter end back to Andrews's big paw. As he took it he said, 'Right. Same with the head rope and bring it down here with you.' When the man handed over the second rope he jumped into the cockpit. Andrews called into the dark behind him. 'OK. Start 'em both, take them up to two thousand seven and hold.' The roar of the big Volvos seemed deafening but when they were steady Andrews called over the noise, 'OK take them down to seven-fifty. Fine.' He flicked the forward rope and it looped off the bollard. He reached forward and turned the big metal wheel and moved it down to full port. Then he shouted, 'OK. OK. Ease in starboard engine.' Immediately the boat's nose was turning and he unlooped the stern rope and they were heading through 180 degrees. 'Right. Both engines now at a thousand.' And the big boat was cutting through the sea. Andrews turned to Felinski. 'We've got

155

separate controls down there. We might need 'em if we get a farewell party.' Then he turned back and released the wheel. There was a big Sestrel compass at the steering position and as Andrews took another look at the chart he was muttering out loud, 'Two-twenty true, two-thirty magnetic.' One of the men came to his shout.'Take over, Frank. Course two-thirty degrees and you can take her gradually up to twenty knots. Shout me when you're there.'

The light on the pier had changed from green to white and an Aldis light blinked a message. When it finished Andrews laughed. 'Cheeky bastards. They signalled to bring them back a shamrock.'

Then they were clear of the shore and the waves were higher and the helmsman was trying to match the speed to the reach of the waves. Andrews came up with a mug in his hand and it slopped and splashed as he gripped a hand-rail. 'They're waiting for you, Steve.'

Felinski went over his rough plan and then answered their questions. The guard reported that the girl was sea-sick and wasn't going to be any trouble. Then the signals corporal shouted to Felinski. He went to where the big receiver was bolted to the bulkhead and the signalman plugged in a spare headphone set to the double jack-plug. They had just finished the news headlines and started the first news item.

'In Moscow today Sir Piers Lake, the British Ambassador, was called to the Soviet Foreign Ministry where a complaint was made that the British authorities were subjecting Soviet Embassy officials in London to systematic harassment. The Foreign Office were not prepared to comment until the complaint had been studied.'

The second item was longer. It covered clashes between strike pickets and police in Birmingham, Manchester, Glasgow and London. Seventy-five arrests had been made and nine policemen had been seriously injured. The deputy leaders of four large unions had warned the Government that a general strike was being considered. The TUC executive had met for four hours in London, and unofficial sources had reported that the major unions had threatened disaffiliation if the executive did not give its blessing to a general strike in forty-eight hours. The Prime Minister was to talk on TV the next evening and appealed

156

for moderate opinion to prevail. He had been referred to as a 'traitor' by a trades union representative on the 'Today's World' programme.

Felinski went back to the cockpit and now there was a long white wake behind them. Andrews handed the binoculars to Felinski. 'We're making good time, there's the light on Haulbowline Rock.' And as the binoculars wandered up and down Felinski finally caught snatched glimpses of a grey granite tower, and a quick triple flash.

The signal corporal came back with a slip of paper. 'Message for you, sir.'

It just said 'FELINSKI STOP SIS WILL RESPOND AS REQUESTED STOP'. That meant that he could get the girl away. They would bring up a vehicle from Dublin to Howth.

There was rain in the air now and the two big Kent Clearviews were whirling round to give some forward vision. Andrews shouted in his ear. 'This rain's a bloody nuisance but it'll be just the job coming into Howth. There'll be nobody about in this lot.'

The outlook cleared when they were off Drogheda and Andrews settled his binoculars to his eyes as best he could. 'Yes, it's Drogheda all right, I can see the framework of the beacon. They've got the three red lights up at the bar. Must be running foul there from the Boyne. That means there'll be nobody out of there for hours yet.' He reached over to the rack alongside the wheel and lifted out the hand-bearing compass and stood swaying with his legs straddled as he took a bearing. 'Helmsman, lay her well off-shore, we want to keep clear of Cardy Rocks and we don't need to come in for Rockabill, they've got a Diaphone. With this offshore blow we should hear it.' And so they did. Four blasts every minute. The wind was backing and falling off but the sea was still running fast and the boat was thundering as the two massive Volvos kept shoving her head into the long rolling waves. Her nose came up as the screws gripped the solid water and she would plane and then crash down as half the screws came clear of the water. Andrews shouted to the relief helmsman to cut the speed. He turned to Felinski. 'We've made good time and we can afford to come down a bit. It's this sort of sea that strains a GRP hull. Starts corkscrewing a bit.'

157

Felinski went down the companionway steps and through to the port cabin. The girl was lying on the bunk but there was some colour in her cheeks. She held a Kleenex to her mouth and her clothes were stained. He sat on the edge of the bunk.

'How are you feeling now?'

She shook her head. 'Terrible.'

'We'll soon be there and it'll go then.'

She leaned up on one elbow and wiped her mouth. She looked at Felinski's face and after a few moments she put out her hand to touch his, and said, 'If I tell you something, will you promise not to harm the Dutchman?'

'How can I promise that? If he gets in the way he's going to get hurt.' It seemed incongruous to Felinski. The girl was deep in a plot to bring England to civil war, moving at ease with murderers and blackmailers, unconcerned at kidnapping, but on the plane she had needed to hold his arm because she was frightened, and now she stroked his hand to comfort and reassure herself that she was still with human beings who might show mercy. Sleeping with odd men as a reward for co-operation.

She spoke again. 'Will it help if I co-operate with you?'

'It would be wise of you to do that anyway, Miss Mathews.'

'But will you kill him?'

'There's no need to kill anyone unless they make trouble.'

'She's your girl, isn't she?'

'Yes.'

'But what I could tell you will help. Maybe you could help your friend.'

Felinski smiled. 'She's not just a friend.'

'I didn't mean the girl. I meant the man.'

'What man?'

'I think his name is Voronov.'

Felinski's voice was harsh. 'What do you know about Voronov?'

'I know that he's done a deal with Ulyanenko.'

'What deal?'

'A deal about the girl.'

'Tell me.'

'Will you keep Jan safe?'

He shook his head. 'Depends what he does.'

'Will you let me speak to him if there's a chance? He won't fight if I say not.'

'If it's possible, OK. But no promises. Now what about the deal.'

'The deal was that the girl wouldn't be killed. Voronov phoned the Embassy and spoke to Ulyanenko.'

'And what's the rest of the deal?'

'That Voronov goes back to Moscow. He told them Yasnov was dead and he offered himself. They want a scapegoat. I think they would blame him publicly for anything that went wrong with the operation in England. Put him on trial or something like that. Say he was mentally ill and was acting on his own. He used some phrase – enemy of something or other.'

'Enemy of the State?'

'Yes, that was it.'

'Where is Voronov now?'

'I've no idea. I don't think *they* know. He's going to wait till he knows the girl is safe. Then he gives himself up. They seemed very pleased with the deal. That's all I know.'

So Yasnov was dead. It didn't take many guesses to know what had happened there. And Voronov had realized that without Yasnov in Moscow the KGB would automatically kill the girl. He wondered whether Franks had realized that, when Yasnov was put down. He wondered what it was like being Franks, consoling the parents knowing that you had virtually written off their child. And Voronov. What had he thought? The man who had changed sides too often. What had motivated *him*? A strange mixture of man, who had no scruples about killing, and who liked pretty women to the point of mania. A man who didn't collect friends. Lovers yes, but friends no. Maybe he had seen Felinski as the nearest he'd got to a friend. Any way you looked at it, it was a strange, sacrificial thing to do. Felinski wondered fleetingly where Voronov would be holed up. He looked back at the girl on the bunk. With her to use it could make it much easier. There was a different way to play it now.

'I want you to listen carefully to me. If you do what I say there is a chance that nobody will get hurt. If you try any tricks then a lot of people will come to grief one way or another.'

'I'll do what you say if it helps Jan.'

'It helps him all right.'

Felinski went back to the cockpit and as he stepped on to the teak gratings the engines went right down to idling and the boat began to yaw, and then broach to the incoming tide. Andrews was looking through the binoculars and he beckoned Felinski over. 'Steve, I think we could give the harbour a miss, there's a longish cove above Howth, this tide will put us right in there. We only draw six feet and I could be in twenty feet according to the charts. You could use the rubber dinghy. It would mean two trips but it's only about fifty yards. There are no houses, nothing. No chance of being seen. How about it?'

'Whatever you say. You're the boss till we get on land. I think it's not going to take as long as I'd planned.'

Twenty minutes later one of the seamen was standing on the foredeck, and as Andrews shouted he pressed his foot on the winch pad, and the anchor rattled out and down. The boat swung round in a wide arc and as they faced the tide the winch motor rumbled and they took up some of the slack. Andrews ordered over the stern anchor and the swinging movement reduced.

Andrews was staying on board and he held the dinghy ropes as five of them, including Felinski and the girl, clambered in. Then they pushed away and the tide took them off. One of the seamen was using one of the oars as a rudder. There was no need to row. They disappeared into the darkness. It was nearly twenty minutes before the dinghy was back for the rest of the party. It was hard work pulling against the tide.

Felinski had settled them in the shelter of two big gorses and he spoke quietly as they listened. 'It's slightly longer this way to the farm but it means we can avoid all the houses in the village. Where the road turns off towards the farm there's a phone box. The girl and I will stop there. We shall give you fifteen minutes to get in position around the farm. Tim will be in charge of that party. When the fifteen minutes are up, the girl will phone the farm. The object is to get van Rijk out of the farm to the phone box. If we can make him play we shall go back to the farm with him, and you'll see us, and see the lights go on. Keep the front door and the back door covered outside. The rest of you come in the farm-house. I'll tell you what to do when you're inside. One of you should check what vehicles there are. You might need one. There's sometimes a van there. That would be ideal. Any questions?'

One of the soldiers asked, 'What do we do if outside people come? The Gardai, or the farm people's mates?'

'We take them and carry on. But we shall leave them behind when we go.'

They were at the phone box in twenty minutes and they synchronized watches and the main party left. There was a shallow ditch alongside the road and Felinski signalled the girl to sit there. He opened the door of the phone box and picked up the receiver. The phone was in order. There was a dialling tone.

He sat by the girl and looked again at his watch. Only a minute gone. The girl was sitting with the light-coloured coat hung loosely round her shoulders and he could feel that she was shivering.

Then the girl was talking of van Rijk. When the operation was finished they had planned to go off together. What would happen now?

As the hand of his watch came up to minus thirty seconds he stood up. He held his hand out for the girl, pulled her to her feet, and then walked with her to the telephone box. As they stood inside he said, 'Remember it protects them all that you do this. I won't harm van Rijk if I can help it.'

She sighed, put in the coins, and dialled the number. He could hear it ringing at the other end. Van Rijk had got to wake and come down to the hall. It was three minutes before the phone clicked and then it was a woman's voice. He snatched the phone from the girl and spoke with the mouthpiece hard against his lips: 'Is van Rijk there?'

There was hesitation at the other end, and then the woman said, 'Who is that?'

'Tell him it's Uly, and it's urgent.'

There was a pause while she considered this and then she said, 'Wait. I'll see.'

Felinski put his hand over the mouthpiece. 'If it's van Rijk who answers I'll pass it to you.'

It was van Rijk.

'Van Rijk, who is that?'

'Jan it's me, Sara. I want to see you quickly. There's some trouble.'

161

'Where are you?'
'At the phone box. Where the lane starts.'
'What's the trouble?'
'Not on the phone love. Just come quickly.'
'OK.'
And the phone clunked down.

It was nearly ten minutes before van Rijk came into sight. He had seen the light colour of the girl's coat and he had walked past, a few yards from where Felinski was standing in the darkness. He'd been smiling as he walked by. He heard the Dutchman laugh as he put his arms round the girl. And he heard the girl's laughing protest as van Rijk pushed her against the phone box. Felinski timed two minutes and then he slid out the pistol and the small torch. It took six strides till he was behind the Dutchman and he said, 'Don't move van Rijk. I've got a gun. Put your hands up slowly.'

Van Rijk had hesitated and then his hands went up level with his head.

'Turn round.'

Felinski shone the torch so that the Dutchman could see the pistol and so that the light was on his face. It was a tough, leathery face but good-looking. Attractive to women. There was a touch of André Previn somewhere.

'Van Rijk, if you do what I tell you nobody will get hurt. If you play games, everybody'll get hurt.'

The hard face looked at him and then the man said, 'What is it you want?'

'We'll go back to the farm. I'll tell you when we get there. I'd better warn you that my men are already there. So take it easy.'

As they moved off van Rijk didn't even glance at the girl. At the entrance to the farm Ted was standing in the shadow of a big elm. His sub-machine gun was pointing towards van Rijk. 'We've cut the telephone line, sir.'

Felinski nodded and they could hear the dogs barking angrily as they walked down the rutted lane to the farm-house.

Joe was at the front door but he only nodded as they went in. There was a good-looking woman in a dressing-gown, holding the phone. She put it down as they came in. She stared from her husband to Felinski, and then to the girl.

'What in heaven's name is all this, Jan?'

It was Felinski who spoke. 'Where is the girl, Mrs van Rijk?'

She looked at her husband but he said nothing.

Felinski waited in the silence and then the others came in.

'Tim, don't get between me and these two. Find Lavender.'

He heard MacNay pound up the stairs. There were heavy footfalls and then the splintering of wood. A few minutes later he heard her say, 'Oh, Steve,' but he didn't look away from the van Rijks.

'Tim, take over from me. Have two of your chaps guard these two and Miss Mathews. I'm going to have a look around.'

At the end of an hour they had loaded the one-ton van with the two radio sets, a bag of one-time code pads and six box-files crammed with typed papers. The piles of arms in the barn were stacked to burn and the barn doused with petrol. They left it fused to go up in two hours. A bag was packed for the van Rijks.

The SIS car and the driver were waiting at the phone box with the lights out.

As Felinski gave his last-minute instructions to MacNay, he said, 'Don't let them stay in Belfast, take them back to London as quickly as you can. Hand them over to Franks, but warn him that it may create problems if he charges them straight away.'

They'd gone off in the van, and he was standing with the girl in the lane. He turned quickly and put his hands on her shoulders. She was thinner in the face and the faint light of dawn made her look white, but as he looked she smiled. 'Are you all right, love?' She nodded, 'Yes, I'm tired and I'm hungry. They're funny people these – fanatics – a bit sick really.'

'Come on. Let's get you back to civilization.'

It was pouring hard when they stood under the glass canopy at the entrance to the Shelbourne, and Felinski had a word with the SIS man. The reception clerk took their dirty clothes in his stride.

Felinski sat in one of the chintzy chairs as she undressed. She sat naked, pink,and lovely, and as she touched her hair she said, 'Did we really do all those things to the Irish that they go on about?'

'Yes, I'm afraid we did. But it was a long time ago.'

She looked across at him smiling. 'Are you going to make love to me, Steve?'

'If you'll let me.'

'Seems funny that I have to get kidnapped before this happens.'

'Right now phone your parents while I have a bath. And when you speak to your old man ask how soon he can marry us. Days not weeks.'

Back in his own room Felinski called the Dublin Embassy, and arranged for them to bring him clothes later that day. And he wanted clothes for the girl too. What did he want, they asked. 'A sweater. She's size fourteen but I'd guess the sweater's size twelve. Blue jeans and pants, and two pairs of shoes.'

Then he phoned Franks and told him about Voronov. 'Any ideas at all where he might be, Steve?'

'He'll be somewhere with a girl, but beyond that I've no ideas at all. I'll call again when I've slept.'

Franks didn't mention the operation.

Felinski leaned back in the warm water and rested his heels on the taps. When he awoke the girl was standing, smiling and looking at him.

'Stephen Felinski, we can be married in ten days. My parents send you their love and I'm waiting impatiently to give you mine. So stop looking at me and come to bed.'

Chapter 23

In the apartment and offices at Curzon Street the files and dossiers had been signed for, and removed to the office of the Director of Public Prosecutions.

Four men sat around a table in the main office room. They were discussing the possibility of arranging the defection of a Soviet scientist who was working on the very big Tokama installation at Kiev. Nuclear fusion was now the highest-grade area of security and science. The Soviets were ahead of the British and the Americans. There were indications of homosexuality in Professor Levkin's background and the four were debating the relative advantages of temptation or blackmail. It seemed likely that the British compromise would be adopted. Temptation and blackmail.

Governors of a number of HM prisons were composing letters to the Home Office on the subject of overcrowding.

The Attorney-General was on a courtesy visit to his old chambers and it was considered to be rather tactless when one of his former colleagues, now gracing the Opposition back benches, had asked about the flood of detainees in various prisons who had not been charged.

Sir Max was a man who always looked as if he were about to smile. It was actually due to cheap dentistry, but it did give him an entirely unearned reputation for giving a friendly hearing to all points of view. Defensively, he had picked up the nearest volume to hand, and now he was jabbing at the big mahogany desk with *Salmon on Torts* as he said, 'We're going through the machinery now, my boy. Most of them we shall do on conspiracy. Expensive trials but longer sentences.'

'The unions aren't going to like it.'

Sir Max laughed and nodded. 'Of course not, of course not. They should have done something about it long ago. The country gave them a good run for their money. They weren't going to stand it for ever, you know. I hear you've been approached by some groups as defence counsel. Should do the chambers a lot of good. I'll be prosecuting myself.'

The Irish Ambassador to the Court of St James had had a flea in his ear from the Foreign Secretary in person. And Miss Sara Mathews had been released into his care on condition that she returned to the Republic immediately. Her diplomatic passport would not, in future, be acceptable to HM Government.

In Dublin the British Ambassador was getting a flea in *his* ear from the Minister of Foreign Affairs himself. It was only after vague threats of the breaking-off of diplomatic relations between the Republic and the UK that he had proffered the two brown files. The Minister had looked down the contents list of each, and turned white first, then red. One was a report on the activities of the Soviet Embassy in Dublin, and the second was a report on the activities of the KGB in England, as operated from the Republic. They were not full reports but they were enough.

The Minister raised his bushy eyebrows as he looked over his glasses at His Excellency. 'I'll pass these on to the right quarters, George. I always said we ought never to have let the buggers set up shop here anyway.'

In Washington the President was sitting at the desk in the oval room. His dinner jacket was hung over the back of his chair, his black tie was undone, and the two ends hung down forlornly alongside the frill on his shirt. The man who sat opposite to him was a big man who filled the slender-legged, gold-painted chair. There were faint echoes of music from the ballroom, just enough to distinguish 'The Yellow Rose of Texas'. The President put down his glass smiling. 'They're playing our tune, Joe.' The big man nodded, and then got up and closed the inner door. As he returned to the chair he said, 'I'd rather be goin' back to Austin than Moscow, Mister President.'

'Do another year, Joe, just to tide us over. Then come back to Washington – or back home to Mary if that's what you want.'

166

The President put his head on one side and looked at the whisky in his glass. 'How did they take it, Joe?'

'Well I was able to speak to Semichastny informally at a party. At the British Embassy. He was pretty worried. I gather there's been some heads rolling. But not so many as there would have been if we had spilled the beans. He gave me the usual bullshit, but they're backing off – there's no doubt about that. He was as near grateful as that kind of bastard can be. The British had their little word with Brezhnev about KGB activities in Britain, and I followed up with a hint about you visiting Moscow next summer. He took it up there and then, and I brought the official invitation over when I came. It's in the Secretary of State's office right now.'

'What's your assessment now, Joe?'

The chair creaked as His Excellency the American Ambassador to the Soviet Union shifted his weight. He wasn't physically uncomfortable, it was no more than a subconscious desire to avoid an answer. But the eyes of the man behind the desk were on him and his answer was awaited.

'I think, Mister President, that although the Presidium don't know that the KGB and the Army were playing games they sense that the *détente* was in danger. So far as the Soviet Union is concerned, I think we tread carefully and tactfully, but if they step out of line anywhere, we should snap back immediately. I think, too, that some little gesture – I had in mind an exchange of medical research – would be very valuable.'

'And the British?'

'That's more Tom's bit than mine, sir.'

The President smiled. 'It was you I asked, Joe. I've heard Tom's views.'

The big man pursed his lips and rubbed his chin.

'Well, they were prepared to break off diplomatic relations with the Soviets – as much to help us as themselves. They've got a lot of trouble-makers in jail. It should be plain sailing. But I just don't know, they let the unions take 'em by the throat. They came to the edge of civil war. Frankly they depress me. I feel they never really recovered from World War Two. They're waiting for a leader and they're making it inevitable that he'll be a dictator. I must sound like Joe Kennedy but that's how I feel.'

167

The President stood up and walked his guest to the door. 'Come and see me before you go back.'

The press reports of the fire at O'Malley's Farm had, for once, been factual. There was no need for exaggeration. The whole of the farm and outlying buildings had been burnt to the ground. Local rumour had it that the twisted remains of guns had been found and that exploding ammunition had spread the fire and kept it ablaze.

Two of the Dublin papers had interviewed the owners, Mr and Mrs van Rijk, who had just returned from a short business trip to London. And they confirmed that the premises had not been insured. There were some who said that it had been insured up to the hilt, but the insurance company had refused all claims because of the guns being on the premises. They said it had been insured in London.

Franks, at his house in Surrey, had been looking out of the French windows, staring across the lawns to where a heap of autumn leaves was still burning, the smoke twisting and turning in the uncertain wind. There had been little praise for the time he had given up. Their minds were already on the next problem. Thank God that this time it had no links with *his* past. He wondered how Felinski and the girl would settle down. Tomorrow the Frau Karl Drusckke would come up. He'd given it its chance but it was uncontrollable. Despite what the rose books said, it wasn't just prolific, rampant was more the word really.

Felinski had taken over from the American. The figures were good. The concrete approach road looked great, and a reluctant Ministry had had its arm twisted by the American to put in a high-grade mixing-mill. But the farm seemed empty and forlorn. Thank God he was spending the evening at the rectory. The lights were on in the rearing house and he walked over. As he went up the concrete steps he could hear the shrill noise of eight thousand week-old chicks. As he opened the door there was absolute silence. He closed it behind him and stood looking at the small yellow birds. A bold one cheeped, then another and soon the air was filled with their noise again, as they scratched and darted among the feeders and the water-cans. The big Calor gas brooders hung over them like steel umbrellas. He stepped over one of the walls of corrugated paper that kept the chicks in the circle of warmth. As he knelt down the small creatures crowded round him and a hero hopped on to his hand. In five minutes he was a farmer again. He just wanted Lavender inside the warm circle with him.

When the dinner was over they'd all been aware that he was on edge. But the world he had been in was not within their compass. There was nothing they could say. But young Lavender Coombs knew what to say, and when she was in the kitchen with her mother she had said, 'I'm going back with Steve to the farm tonight.'

'Well that's fine, dear.'

'No, I mean I'm going to stay there with him till we get married.' Then she saw the tears in her mother's eyes. They didn't fall but if she blinked they'd fall. Lavender knew all about those sort of tears. 'Don't cry, mother. I'll be fine.'

Her mother reached out and touched her face. 'I was thinking about Steve, love. You'll be all right. I worry about him. I think the war messed him about.'

And then they were both crying but it was good cathartic crying. Wedding morning crying.

The air correspondents of the *Daily Express* and the *Daily Telegraph* were exchanging slanderous comments about their respective editors as they stamped their feet in the frosty cold of London Airport. It was the second flight from London of the Russians' Concorde – officially, as always, the TU-144, but to the Press and the public it would always be Concordski. The plane that had left Bristol way behind.

Like others of the fourth estate they'd been tipped off that it was an important flight to Moscow. Hints that there would be a journalistic reward in the future. But it was all hints and no facts. The Soviet Press Officer was not one for hot tips, not even cold tips.

The four Kuznetsov turbo-jets were idling with a noise like thunder. The crew had gone aboard twenty minutes before, and at the foot of the gangway were four men in dark winter coats and felt hats, which they were holding on their heads against the wind and the slipstream. Then there was a stir and a big man walked across the tarmac. He wore a grey coat and no hat. He had sparse curly blond hair and an ugly smiling face. About halfway to the plane he turned towards the terminal buildings, stopped, and looked up at the glass gallery. The correspondents looked up too and they saw a very pretty girl waving to the man. She had a bunch of red roses in her other hand. They looked back to the big man. He had a rose in the buttonhole of his coat. One of the four men by the plane shouted something to him in Russian. The man half turned and, after examining the group carefully, made a very British gesture to them with two fingers. He turned back to the girl and kissed both hands to her. He was grinning. Then he turned on his heel, pulled up his coat-collar and walked to the aircraft steps. He didn't turn or wave again, and the four men followed behind him closely up the gangway. It was wheeled away as the cabin door was swung to. It was time for everyone to go home.